Petunia:
Never Despair

Senator Alan MacGregor was
determined to win his bid for
Shelby Campbell's heart. She
had vowed never to love and
lose another politician, but
Alan was prepared to prove
that dreams come true for
those who never despair....

NORA ROBERTS

LANGUAGE OF LOVE

Love has a language all its own, and for
centuries flowers have symbolized
love's finest expression.
Discover the language of flowers
—and love—
in this romantic collection of 48 favorite
books by bestselling author Nora Roberts.

1. Lily of the Valley
   IRISH THOROUGHBRED
2. Hollyhock THE LAW IS A LADY
3. Cabbage Rose IRISH ROSE
4. Wallflower STORM WARNING
5. Foxglove FIRST IMPRESSIONS
6. Yellow Jasmine REFLECTIONS
7. Marigold NIGHT MOVES
8. Narcissus DANCE OF DREAMS
9. China Aster OPPOSITES ATTRACT
10. Amaryllis ISLAND OF FLOWERS
11. Great Yellow Daffodil
    SEARCH FOR LOVE
12. Hyacinth PLAYING THE ODDS
13. Gloxinia TEMPTING FATE
14. Forget-me-not FROM THIS DAY
15. Petunia ALL THE POSSIBILITIES
16. Tuberose HEART'S VICTORY
17. Red Poppy ONE MAN'S ART
18. Gladiola RULES OF THE GAME
19. White Periwinkle
    FOR NOW, FOREVER
20. Pansy HER MOTHER'S KEEPER
21. Orchid PARTNERS
22. Stock SULLIVAN'S WOMAN
23. Dahlia SUMMER DESSERTS
24. Iris THIS MAGIC MOMENT
25. Pink LESSONS LEARNED
26. Lavender THE RIGHT PATH
27. Love in a Mist
    THE ART OF DECEPTION
28. Azalea UNTAMED
29. Red Carnation DUAL IMAGES
30. Bluebell SECOND NATURE
31. Red and White Roses
    ONE SUMMER
32. Wisteria GABRIEL'S ANGEL
33. Trumpet Flower
    THE NAME OF THE GAME
34. Purple Columbine
    A WILL AND A WAY
35. Honeysuckle AFFAIRE ROYALE
36. Spring Crocus
    LESS OF A STRANGER
37. Crown Imperial
    COMMAND PERFORMANCE
38. White Camellia BLITHE IMAGES
39. Cyclamen THE PLAYBOY PRINCE
40. Purple Lilac TREASURES LOST,
    TREASURES FOUND
41. White Daisy RISKY BUSINESS
42. Red Tulip LOVING JACK
43. Apple Blossom TEMPTATION
44. Dogwood BEST LAID PLANS
45. Clematis MIND OVER MATTER
46. Garden Anemone THE WELCOMING
47. Snapdragon BOUNDARY LINES
48. Morning Glory LOCAL HERO

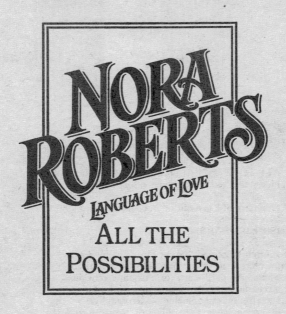

NORA ROBERTS

LANGUAGE OF LOVE

ALL THE POSSIBILITIES

Silhouette Books®

SILHOUETTE BOOKS
300 East 42nd St., New York, N.Y. 10017

ALL THE POSSIBILITIES © 1985 by Nora Roberts.
First published as a Silhouette Special Edition.

Language of Love edition published August 1991.

ISBN: 0-373-51015-2

Printed in U.S.A.

Chapter One

Shelby knew Washington was a crazy town. That's why she loved it. She could have elegance and history, if that's what she wanted, or dingy clubs and burlesque. On a trip from one side of town to the other, she could go from grace and style to mean streets—there was always a choice: gleaming white monuments, dignified state buildings, old brick row houses, steel and glass boxes; statues that had oxidized too long ago to remember what they'd oxidized from; cobblestoned streets or Watergate.

But the city hadn't been built around one particular structure for nothing. The Capitol was the core, and politics was always the name of the game. Washington bustled frantically—not with the careless ongoing rush of New York, but with a wary, look-over-your-shoulder sort of frenzy. For the bulk of the men and women who worked there, their jobs were on the line from election to election. One thing Washington was not, was a blanket of security. That's why Shelby loved it. Security equaled complacency and complacency equaled boredom. She'd always made it her first order of business never to be bored.

Georgetown suited her because it was yet it wasn't D.C. It had the energy of youth: the University, boutiques, coffee houses, half-price beer on Wednesday nights. It had the dignity of age: residential streets, ivied red brick walls, painted shutters, neat women walking neat dogs. Because it couldn't be strictly labeled as part of something else, she was comfortable there. Her shop faced out on one of the narrow cobblestoned streets with her living quarters on the second floor. She had a balcony, so she could sit out on warm summer nights and listen to the city move. She had bamboo slats at the windows so she could have privacy if she chose. She rarely did.

Shelby Campbell had been made for people, for conversations and crowds. Strangers were just as fascinating to talk to as old friends, and noise was more appealing than silence. Still, she liked to live at her own pace, so her roommates weren't of the human sort. Moshe Dayan was a one-eyed tomcat, and Auntie Em was a parrot who refused to converse with anyone. They lived together in relative peace in the cluttered disorder Shelby called home.

She was a potter by trade and a merchant by whim. The little shop she had called Calliope had become a popular success in the three years since she'd opened the doors. She'd found she enjoyed dealing with customers almost as much as she enjoyed sitting at her potter's wheel with a lump of clay and her imagination. The paperwork was a matter of constant annoyance. But then, to Shelby, annoyances gave life its bite. So, to her family's amusement and the surprise of many friends, she'd gone into trade and made an undeniable success of it.

At six, she locked the shop. From the outset, Shelby had made a firm policy not to give her evenings to her business. She might work with clay or glazes until the early hours of the morning, or go out and mix with the street-life, but the merchant in her didn't believe in overtime. Tonight, however, she faced something she avoided whenever possible and took completely seriously when she couldn't: an obligation. Switching off lights as she went, Shelby climbed the stairs to the second floor.

The cat leapt nimbly from his perch on the windowsill, stretched and padded toward her. When Shelby came in, dinner wasn't far behind. The bird fluffed her wings and began to gnaw on her cuttlebone.

"How's it going?" She gave Moshe an absent scratch behind the ears where he liked it best. With a sound of approval, he looked up at her with his one eye, tilting his head so that the patch he wore looked raffish and right. "Yeah, I'll feed you." Shelby pressed a hand to her own stomach. She was starving, and the best she could hope for that evening would be liver wrapped in bacon and crackers.

"Oh, well," she murmured as she went into the kitchen to feed the cat. She'd promised her mother she'd make an appearance at Congressman Write's cocktail party, so she was stuck. Deborah Campbell was probably the only one capable of making Shelby feel stuck.

Shelby was fond of her mother, over and above the basic love of a child for her parent. There were times they were taken for sisters, despite the twenty-five-year difference in their ages. The coloring was the same—bright red hair too fiery for chestnut, too dark for titian. While her mother wore hers short and sleek, Shelby let hers curl naturally with a frizz of bangs that always seemed just a tad too long. Shelby had inherited her mother's porcelain complexion and smoky eyes, but whereas the combination made Deborah look delicately elegant, Shelby somehow came across looking more like a waif who'd sell flowers on a streetcorner. Her face was narrow, with a hint of bone and hollow. She often exploited her image with a clever hand at makeup and an affection for antique clothes.

She might have inherited her looks from her mother, but her personality was hers alone. Shelby never thought about being freewheeling or eccentric, she simply was. Her background and upbringing were lodged in Washington, and overtones of politics had dominated her childhood. Election-year pressure, the campaign trail that had taken her father away from home for weeks at a time, lobbying, bills to pass or block—they were all part of her past.

There'd been careful children's parties that had been as much a part of the game as a press conference. The children of Senator Robert Campbell were important to his image—an image that had been carefully projected as suitable for the Oval Office. And a great deal of the image, as Shelby remembered, had been simple fact. He'd been a good man, fair-minded, affectionate, dedicated, with a keen sense of the ridiculous. That hadn't saved him from a madman's bullet fifteen years before.

She'd made up her mind then that politics had killed her father. Death came to everyone—even at eleven, she'd understood that. But it had come too soon for Robert Campbell. And if it could strike him, who she'd imagined was invulnerable, it could strike anyone, anytime. Shelby had decided with all the fervor of a young child to enjoy every moment of her life and to squeeze it for everything there was to have. Since then, nothing had changed her analysis. So, she'd go to Write's cocktail party at his spacious home across the river and find something there to amuse or interest her. Shelby never doubted she'd succeed.

Shelby was late, but then, she always was. It wasn't from any conscious carelessness or need to make an entrance. She was always late because she never finished anything as quickly as she thought she would. Besides, the white brick Colonial was crowded, filled with enough people that a latecomer wasn't noticed.

The room was as wide as Shelby's entire apartment and twice as long. It was done in whites and ivories and creams, which added to the sense of uncluttered space. A few excellent French landscapes hung on the walls in ornate frames. Shelby approved the ambience, though she couldn't have lived with it herself. She liked the scent of the place—tobaccos, mixed perfumes and colognes, the faintest trace of light sweat. It was the aroma of people and parties.

Conversations were typical of most cocktail parties— clothes, other parties, golf scores—but running through it were murmurs on the price index, the current NATO talks, and the Secretary of the Treasury's recent interview on "Face to Face."

Shelby knew most of the people there, dressed in thin silks or in tailored dark suits. She evaded capture by any of them with quick smiles and greetings as she worked her way with practiced skill to the buffet. Food was one thing she took very seriously. When she spotted finger-sized quiches, she decided her evening wasn't going to be a total loss after all.

"Why, Shelby, I didn't even know you were here. How nice to see you." Carol Write, looking quietly elegant in mauve linen, had slipped through the crowd without spilling a drop of her sherry.

"I was late," Shelby told her, returning the brief hug with her mouth full. "You have a beautiful home, Mrs. Write."

"Why, thank you, Shelby. I'd love to give you a tour a little later if I can slip away." She gave a quick, satisfied glance around at the crowd—the banner of a Washington hostess. "How are things at your shop?"

"Fine. I hope the congressman's well."

"Oh, yes. He'll want to see you—I can't tell you how much he loves that urn you made for his office." Though she had a soft Georgian drawl, Carol could talk as quickly as a New York shopkeeper making a pitch. "He still says it was the best birthday present I ever bought him. Now, you must mingle." Carol had Shelby's elbow before she could grab another quiche. "No one's better at keeping conversations moving than you are. Too much shop talk can simply murder a party. There are several people here you know of course, but—ah, here's Deborah. I'll just leave you to her a moment and play hostess."

Released, Shelby eased back toward the buffet. "Hello, Mama."

"I was beginning to think you'd backed out." Deborah skimmed a glance over her daughter, marveling that the rainbow-colored skirt, peasant blouse, and bolero looked so right on her when it would have been a costume on anyone else.

"Um-um, I promised." Shelby cast a connoisseur's eye over the buffet before she made her next choice. "Food's better than I expected."

"Shelby, get your mind off your stomach." With a half sigh, Deborah hooked arms with her daughter. "In case you haven't noticed, there are several nice young men here."

"Still trying to marry me off?" Shelby kissed her lightly on the cheek. "I'd almost forgiven you for the pediatrician you tried to foist on me."

"He was a very personable young man."

"Hmmm." Shelby decided not to mention that the personable young man had had six pairs of hands—all very active.

"Besides, I'm not trying to marry you off; I just want you to be happy."

"Are you happy?" Shelby countered with a quick gleam in her eye.

"Why, yes," Absently Deborah tightened the diamond stud in her left ear. "Of course I am."

"When are you going to get married?"

"I've *been* married," Deborah reminded her with a little huff. "I've had two children, and—"

"Who adore you. I've got two tickets for the ballet at the Kennedy Center next week. Want to come with me?"

The faint frown of annoyance vanished from Deborah's brow. How many women, she thought, had a daughter who could exasperate and please so fully at the same time? "A clever way to change the subject, and I'd love to."

"Can I come to dinner first?" she asked, then beamed a smile to her left. "Hi, Steve." She tested a solid upper arm. "You've been working out."

Deborah watched her offspring spill charm over the Assistant Press Secretary, then dole out more to the newly appointed head of the EPA without missing a beat. Effortless, genuine, Deborah mused. No one enjoyed, or was enjoyed by a crowd, so much as Shelby. Then, why did she so scrupulously avoid the one-on-one entanglements? If it had been simply marriage that Shelby avoided, Deborah would have accepted it, but for a long time, she'd suspected it was something else Shelby blocked off.

Deborah would never have wished her daughter unhappiness, but even that would have relieved her mind. She'd watched Shelby avoid emotional pain one way or another for fifteen years. Without pain, Deborah knew, there was never true fulfillment. Yet... she sighed when Shelby laughed that smoky careless laugh as she drew out various members of the group she'd joined. Yet Shelby was so vital, so bright. Perhaps she was worrying over nothing. Happiness was a very personal thing.

Alan watched the woman with flaming hair who was dressed like a wealthy Gypsy. He could hear her laugh float across the room, at once sensuous and innocent. An interesting face, he mused, more unique than beautiful. What was she? he wondered. Eighteen? Thirty? She didn't seem to belong to a Washington party—God knows he'd been at enough of them to know who did. There was nothing sleek or cautious about her. That dress hadn't come from one of the accepted shops the political wives patronized, and her hair certainly hadn't been styled in any sophisticated salon. But she fit in. Despite the touch of L.A. flair and New York savvy, she fit right in. But who the hell—

"Well, Senator." Write gave Alan a firm slap on the back. "It's good to see you outside the arena. We don't lure you out often enough."

"Good Scotch, Charlie." Alan lifted his glass again. "It always does the trick."

"It usually takes more than that," Write corrected. "You burn a lot of midnight oil, Alan."

Alan smiled easily. No one's moves were secret in Washington. "There seems to be a lot to burn at the moment."

With a nod for agreement, Write sipped his drink. "I'm interested in your views on Breiderman's bill coming up next week."

Alan met the congressman's eyes calmly, knowing Write was one of Breiderman's leading supporters. "I'm against it," he said simply. "We can't afford any more cuts in education."

"Well, Alan, you and I know things aren't so black and white."

"Sometimes the gray area gets too large—then it's best to go back to basics." He didn't want a debate, and he discovered he didn't want shop talk. It was a poor mood to be in for a senator at a political party. But Alan MacGregor was enough politician to evade questions when it suited him. "You know, I thought I knew everyone here." Alan glanced idly around the room. "The woman who seems to be a cross between Esmeralda and Heidi—who is she?"

"Who?" Write repeated, intrigued enough by the description to forget his planned retort and follow Alan's gaze. "Oh, don't tell me you haven't met Shelby." He grinned, enjoying the description more now that he knew whom it referred to. "Want an introduction?"

"I think I'll handle it myself," Alan murmured. "Thanks."

Alan wandered away, moving easily through the groups of people, stopping when pressed to. Like Shelby, he was made for crowds. Handshakes, smiles, the right word at the right time, a good memory for faces. It was stock-in-trade for a man whose career hinged on public whim as much as on his own skill. And he was skilled.

Alan knew the law; was familiar with all its shades and angles, though unlike his brother, Caine, also a lawyer, Alan had been drawn to the theory of law more than the individual cases. It had been the overview that had fascinated him—how the law, or the basis for it, the Constitution, worked for the people. Politics had caught his imagination in college, and even now at thirty-five; with a term in Congress behind him and his first term in the Senate under way, he enjoyed exploring its endless possibilities.

"Alone, Alan?" Myra Ditmeyer, a Supreme Court Justice's wife, plucked at his arm as he edged away from a group.

Alan grinned and with the privilege of an old friend, kissed her cheek. "Is that an offer?"

She gave one of her booming laughs, shaking so that the ruby drops at her ears danced. "Oh, you devil, if it only could be. Twenty years, you Scottish heartbreaker; all I'd need would be twenty years—a drop in the bucket." Her smile was genuine, her eyes shrewd as she studied him. "Why don't you have one of those polished cosmopolitan types of yours on your arm tonight?"

"I was hoping to talk you into a weekend in Puerto Vallarta."

This time Myra poked a long scarlet nail into his chest as she laughed. "It would serve you right if I took you up on it. You think I'm safe." She sighed, her round, finely lined face falling into wistful lines. "Unfortunately true. We need to find you someone dangerous, Alan Mac-Gregor. A man your age still single." She clucked her tongue. "Americans like their presidents tidily married, my dear."

Alan's grin only widened. "Now you sound like my father."

"That old pirate." Myra sniffed, but a gleam of amusement shone in her eyes. "Still, you'd be wise to take his advice on a thing or two. A successful politician is a couple."

"I should get married to advance my career?"

"Don't try to outsmart me," Myra ordered, then saw his eyes shift in the direction of a low, familiar laugh.

Well, well, she thought, wouldn't that be an interesting match? The fox and the butterfly.

"I'm having a dinner party next week," she decided on the spot. "Just a few friends. My secretary will call your office with the details." Patting his cheek with a many-ringed hand, she moved away to find a strategic spot to watch.

Seeing Shelby drift away from the trio she was talking with, Alan moved in her direction. When he was near, the first thing he noticed was her scent—not floral, not spicy or musk, but a teasing merging of all three. It was more an aura than a perfume, and unforgettable. Shelby had crouched down in front of a curio cabinet, her nose pressed close.

"Eighteenth-century china," she murmured, sensing someone behind her. " 'Tea-dust' glaze. Spectacular, isn't it?"

Alan glanced down at the bowl that seemed to fascinate her, then at the crown of vivid red hair. "It certainly draws attention."

She looked up over her shoulder and smiled—as stunning and unique an allure as her scent. "Hello."

"Hello." He took the hand she held up—strong and hard, a paradox with her looks—and helped her to her feet. He didn't relinquish it as he normally would have done without thinking, but continued to hold it as she smiled up at him.

"I got distracted on my way to my objective. Would you do me a favor?"

His brow lifted. There was a ring of both finishing school and the streets in her speech. "What?"

"Just stand here." In a swift move, she steered around him, slipped a plate off the buffet, and began to fill it. "Every time I start to do this, someone sees me and hauls me off. I missed my dinner. There." Satisfied, she nudged

Alan's arm. "Let's go out on the terrace." Shelby slipped around the table and through the French doors.

Warm air and the scent of early lilacs. Moonlight fell over grass that had been freshly mowed and tidily raked. There was an old willow with tender new branches that dipped onto the flagstone. With a sigh of pure sensual greed, Shelby popped a chilled shrimp into her mouth. "I don't know what this is," she murmured, giving a tiny hors d'oeuvre a close study. "Have a taste and tell me."

Intrigued, Alan bit into the finger food she held to his mouth. "Pâté wrapped in pastry with . . . a touch of chestnut."

"*Hmm*. Okay." Shelby devoured the rest of it. "I'm Shelby," she told him, setting the plate on a glass table and sitting behind it.

"I'm Alan." A smile lingered on his mouth as he sat beside her. Where did this street waif come from? he wondered. He decided he could spend the time to find out, and the spring air was a welcome relief from the tobacco smoke and hothouse flowers inside. "Are you going to share any of that?"

Shelby studied him as she considered. She'd noticed him across the room, perhaps because he was tall with a naturally athletic build you didn't often see at a Washington party. You saw carefully maintained builds, the kind that spoke of workouts three times a week and racquetball, but his was more like a swimmer's—a channel swimmer's— long and lean. He'd cut through currents with little resistance.

His face wasn't smooth; there were a few lines of care in it that complemented the aristocratic cast of his face and his long, thin mouth. His nose was slightly out of alignment, which appealed to her. The dark hair and dark eyes made her think of a Brontë hero—Heathcliff or Rochester, she wasn't sure. But he had a thoughtful, brooding quality about him that was both restful and distracting. Shelby's lips curved again.

"Sure. I guess you earned it. What are you drinking?"

Alan reached toward the plate. "Scotch, straight up."

"I knew you could be trusted." Shelby took the glass from him and sipped. Her eyes laughed over the rim; the faint breeze played with her hair. Moonlight, starlight, suited her. She looked, for a moment, like an elf who might vanish with a puff at will.

"What are you doing here?" he asked her.

"Maternal pressure," she told him easily. "Have you ever experienced it?"

His smile was wry and appealing. "Paternal pressure is my specialty."

"I don't imagine there's much difference," Shelby decided over a full mouth. Swallowing, she rested the side of her face on her palm. "Do you live in Alexandria?"

"No, Georgetown."

"Really? Where?"

The moonlight glimmered in her eyes, showing him they were as pure a gray as he'd ever seen. "P Street."

"Funny we haven't run into each other in the local market. My shop's only a few blocks from there."

"You run a shop?" Funky dresses, velvet jackets, he imagined. Perhaps jewelry.

"I'm a potter." Shelby pushed his glass back across the table.

"A potter." On impulse, Alan took her hand, turning it over to examine it. Small and narrow, her fingers were long, with the nails clipped short and unpainted. He liked the feel of her hand, and the look of her wrist under a heavy gold bracelet. "Are you any good?"

"I'm terrific." For the first time that she could remember, she had to suppress the urge to break contact. It ran through her mind that if she didn't, he was going to hold her there until she forgot she had other places to go. "You're not a Washington native," she continued, experimenting by letting her hand stay in his. "What is it…New England?"

"Massachusetts. Very good." Sensing the slight resistance in her hand, Alan kept it in his as he picked up another hors d'oeuvre and offered it.

"Ah, the trace of Harvard lingers." So did a slight disdain in her voice. His eyes narrowed fractionally at it. "Not medicine," she speculated as she allowed her fingers to lace with his. It was already becoming a very comfortable sensation. "Your palms aren't smooth enough for medicine."

Perhaps one of the arts? she wondered, again noticing that romantically brooding expression in his eyes. A dreamer, she suspected—a man who tended to think things through layer by layer before he acted.

"Law." Alan accepted the careful study as well as the faint surprise on her face. "Disappointed?"

"Surprised." Although his voice suited the law, she decided—smooth and clean with undercurrents that might have been drama or humor. "But then I suppose my conception of lawyers is at fault. Mine has jowls and wears tortoiseshell glasses. Don't you think the law tends to get in the way of a lot of ordinary things?"

His brow lifted in direct harmony with the corner of his mouth. "Such as murder and mayhem?"

"Those aren't ordinary things—well, maybe mayhem," Shelby corrected as she took another sip from his glass. "I suppose I mean the endless red tape of bureaucracy. Do you know all the forms I have to fill out just to sell my pieces? Then someone has to read those forms, someone else has to file them, and someone else has to send out more when the time comes. Wouldn't it be simpler just to let me sell a vase and make my living?''

''Difficult when you're dealing with millions.'' Alan forgot that he hadn't wanted to debate as he idly toyed with the ring she wore on her pinky. ''Not everyone would adhere to a fair profit balance, no one would pay taxes, and the small businessman would have no more protection than the consumer would.''

''It's hard to believe filling out my social security number in triplicate accomplishes all that.'' His touch moving in a half-friendly, half-seductive manner over her skin was distracting enough, but when he smiled—when he really smiled—Shelby decided he was the most irresistible male she'd ever encountered. Perhaps it was that touch of sobriety lurking around the edges of humor.

''There's always a large overlap between bureaucracy and necessity.'' He wondered—only for a moment—what in hell he was doing having this conversation with a woman who looked like a nineteenth-century waif and smelled like every man's dream.

''The best thing about rules is the infinite variety of ways to break them.'' Shelby gave a trickle of the laughter that had first attracted him. ''I suppose that's what keeps you in business.''

A voice drifted through the open window, brisk, cool, and authoritative. ''Nadonley might have his finger on the pulse of American-Israeli relations, but he isn't making many friends with his current policy.''

''And his frumpy, tourist-class travel look is wearing a bit thin.''

''Typical,'' Shelby murmured, with the shadow of a frown in her eyes. ''Clothes are as political as beliefs—

probably more. Dark suits, white shirt, you're a conservative. Loafers and a cashmere sweater, a liberal.''

He'd heard that slick arrogance toward his profession before—quiet or noisy depending on the occasion. Normally Alan ignored it. This time it irked him. ''You tend to simplify, don't you?''

''Only what I don't have any patience with,'' she acknowledged carelessly. ''Politics've been an annoying by-product of society since before Moses debated with Ramses.''

The smile began to play around his mouth again. Shelby didn't know him well enough yet to realize it was a challenging one. To think he'd nearly given in to the urge to stay home and spend a quiet evening with a book. ''You don't care for politicians.''

''It's one of the few generalizations I'm prone to. They come in several flavors—stuffy, zealot, hungry, shaky. I've always found it frightening that a handful of men run this strange world. So...'' With a shrug, she pushed aside her plate. ''I make it a habit to pretend I really do have control over my own destiny.'' She leaned closer again, enjoying the way the shadows of the willow played over his face. It was tempting to test the shape and feel of it with her fingers. ''Would you like to go back in?''

''No.'' Alan let his thumb trace lightly over her wrist. He felt the quick, almost surprised increase of her pulse. ''I had no idea how bored I was in there until I came out here.''

Shelby's smile was instant and brilliant. ''The highest of compliments, glibly stated. You're not Irish, are you?''

He shook his head, wondering just how that mobile, pixielike mouth was going to taste. ''Scottish.''

''Good God, so am I.'' The shadow crossed her eyes again as a trickle of anticipation ran along her skin. ''I'm beginning to think it's fate. I've never been comfortable with fate."

"Controlling your own destiny?" Giving in to a rare impulse, he lifted her fingers to his lips.

"I prefer the driver's seat," she agreed, but she let her hand linger there, pleasing them both. "The Campbell practicality."

This time it was Alan's turn to laugh, long and with unbridled amusement. "To old feuds," he said, lifting his glass to her. "Undoubtedly our ancestors slaughtered one another to the wailing of bagpipes. I'm of the clan MacGregor."

Shelby grinned. "My grandfather would put me on bread and water for giving you the right time. A damn mad MacGregor." Alan's grin widened while hers slowly faded. "Alan MacGregor," she said quietly. "Senator from Massachusetts."

"Guilty."

Shelby sighed as she rose. "A pity."

Alan didn't relinquish her hand, but stood so that their bodies were close enough to brush, close enough to transmit the instant, complicated attraction. "Why is that?"

"I might have risked my grandfather's fury..." Shelby gave his face another quick study, intrigued by the unsteady rate of her own heart. "Yes, I believe I would have—but I don't date politicians."

"Really?" Alan's gaze lowered to her mouth then came back to hers. He hadn't asked her for one. He understood, and didn't entirely approve, that she was the kind of woman who'd do her own asking when it suited her. "Is that one of Shelby's rules?"

"Yes, one of the few."

Her mouth was tempting—small, unpainted, and faintly curved as if she considered the entire thing a joke on both of them. Yes, her mouth was tempting, but the amusement in her eyes was a challenge. Instead of doing the obvious, Alan brought her hand up and pressed his lips to her wrist, watching her. He felt the quick jerk and scramble of her pulse, saw the wariness touched with heat flicker in her eyes. "The best thing about rules," Alan quoted softly, "is the infinite variety of ways to break them."

"Hoist with my own petard," she murmured as she drew her hand away. It was ridiculous, Shelby told herself, to be unsteady over an old-fashioned romantic gesture. But there was a look in those dark brown eyes that told her he'd done it as much for that purpose as to please himself.

"Well, Senator," she began with a firmer voice, "it's been nice. It's time I put in another appearance inside."

Alan let her get almost to the doors before he spoke. "I'll see you again, Shelby."

She stopped to glance over her shoulder. "It's a possibility."

"A certainty," he corrected.

She narrowed her eyes a moment. He stood near the glass table with the moon at his back—tall, dark, and built for action. His face was very calm, his stance relaxed, yet she had the feeling if she thumbed her nose at him, he could be on her before she'd drawn a breath. That alone nearly tempted her to try it. Shelby gave her head a little toss to send the bangs shifting on her forehead. The half-smile he was giving her was infuriating, especially since it made her want to return it. Without a word, she opened the doors and slipped inside.

That, she told herself, would be the end of that. She very nearly believed it.

Chapter Two

Shelby had hired a part-time shop assistant almost two years before so she'd be free to take an hour or a day off when it suited her mood, or to spend several days at a time if it struck her, with her craft. She'd found her answer in Kyle, a struggling poet whose hours were flexible and whose temperament suited hers. He worked for Shelby regularly on Wednesdays and Saturdays, and for sporadic hours whenever she called him. In return, Shelby paid him well and listened to his poetry. The first nourished his body, the second his soul.

Shelby invariably set aside Saturdays to toss or to turn clay, though she would have been amused if anyone had termed her disciplined: she still thought she worked then because she chose to, not because she'd fallen into a routine. Nor did she fully realize just how much those quiet Saturdays at her wheel centered her life.

Her workroom was at the rear of the shop. There were sturdy shelves lining two walls, crowded with projects that had been fired to biscuit or were waiting for their turn in the kiln. There were rows and rows of glazes—her palette of color—no less important to her than to any artist. There were tools: long wooden-handled needles, varied-shaped brushes, firing cones. Dominating the back wall was a large walk-in kiln, closed now, with its shelves stacked with glazed and decorated pottery in their final firing.

Because the vents were open and the room itself wasn't large, the high temperature of the kiln kept the room sultry. Shelby worked at her wheel in a T-shirt and cutoffs with a white-bibbed apron designed to protect her from most of the splatters.

There were two windows, both opening out on the alley, so she heard little of the weekend street noises. She used the radio for company, and with her hair pulled back by a leather thong, bent over the wheel with the last clay ball she intended to throw that day.

Perhaps she liked this part of her craft the best—taking a lump of clay and forming it into whatever her skill and imagination produced. It might be a vase or a bowl, squat or slender, ridged or smooth. It might be an urn that would have to wait for her to add the handles, or a pot that would one day hold jasmine tea or spiced coffee. Possibilities. Shelby never ceased to be fascinated by them.

The glazing, the adding of color and design, appealed to a different part of her nature. That was finishing work— creative certainly, and taxing. She could be lavish or frugal with color as she chose, using careful detail or bold splashes. Working the clay was more primitive, and therefore more challenging.

With bare hands she would mold and nudge and coax a formless ball of clay to her own will. Shelby realized people often did that to one another, and to their children in particular. She didn't like the idea and focused that aspect of her ego on the clay: she would mold, flatten, and remold until it suited her. She preferred people to be less malleable; molds were for the inanimate. Anyone who fit into one too neatly was already half dead.

She'd worked the air bubbles out of the clay. It was damp and fresh, carefully mixed to give her the right consistency. She added the grog, coarsely ground bits of broken pottery, to increase the stiffness and was ready to begin. The moistened bat was waiting. Using both hands, Shelby pressed the clay down as the wheel began to turn. She held the soft, cool earth firmly in cupped hands until it ran true on the wheel, allowing herself to feel the shape she wanted to create.

Absorbed, she worked with the radio murmuring unheard behind her. The wheel hummed. The clay spun, succumbing to the pressure of her hands, yielding to the unrelenting demands of her imagination. She formed a thick-walled ring, pressing her thumb in the center of the ball, then slowly, very slowly, pulled it upward between her thumb and fingers to form a cylinder. She could flatten it into a plate now, open it into a bowl, perhaps close it into a sphere, according to her own pleasure.

She was both in control and driven. Her hands dominated the clay as surely as her creativity dominated her. She felt the need for something symmetrical, poised. In the back of her mind was a strong image of masculinity—something with clean, polished lines and understated elegance. She began to open the clay, her hands deft and sure, slick now with the reddish-brown material. A bowl became her objective, deep with a wide ridge, along the lines of a Roman krater, handleless. The rotation and the pressure of her hands forced the clay wall up. The shape was no longer only in her mind as she molded the clay inside and out.

With skilled hands and an experienced eye, she molded the shape into proportion, tapering it out for the stem of the base, then flattening. The time and patience she applied here she took for granted, and spared for few other aspects of her life. Only the energy touched all of her.

Shelby could already envision it finished in a dark jade green with hints, but only hints, of something softer beneath the surface of the glaze. No decoration, no fluting or scrolled edges—the bowl would be judged on its shape and strength alone.

When the shape was complete, she resisted the urge to fuss. Too much care was as dangerous as too little. Turning off the wheel, Shelby gave the bowl one long critical study before taking it to the shelf she reserved for drying. The next day, when it was leather-hard, she'd put it back on the wheel and use her tools to refine it, shaving off any unwanted clay. Yes, jade green, she decided. And with careful inglazing, she could produce those hints of softness under the rich, bold tone.

Absently she arched her back, working out the tiny, nagging kinks she hadn't noticed while the wheel was on. A hot bath, Shelby decided, before she went out to join some friends in that new little club on M Street. With a sigh that was as much from satisfaction as weariness, she turned. Then gasped.

"That was quite an education." Alan slipped his hands out of his pockets and crossed to her. "Do you know what shape you're after when you start, or does it come as you're working?"

Shelby blew her bangs out of her eyes before she answered. She wouldn't do the expected and ask him what he was doing there, or how he'd gotten in. "It depends."

She lifted a brow, vaguely surprised to see him in jeans and a sweatshirt. The man she had met the night before had seemed too polished for such casual clothes, especially for denim white at the stress points from wear. The tennis shoes were expensive, but they weren't new. Neither was the gold watch at the end of a subtly muscled arm. Wealth suited him, and yet he didn't seem the sort of man who'd be careless with it. He'd know his own bank balance—something Shelby couldn't claim to—what stocks he owned and their market value.

Alan didn't fidget during the survey. He'd grown too used to being in the public eye to be concerned with any sort of dissection. And, he thought she was entitled to her turn as he'd done little else but stare at her for the last thirty minutes.

"I suppose I should say I'm surprised to see you here, Senator, since I am." A hint of amusement touched her mouth. "And since I imagine you intended for me to be."

In acknowledgement, he inclined his head. "You work hard," he commented, glancing down at her clay-coated hands. "I've always thought artists must burn up as much energy as athletes when the adrenaline's flowing. I like your shop."

"Thanks." Because the compliment had been simple and genuine, Shelby smiled fully. "Did you come in to browse?"

"In a manner of speaking." Alan resisted the urge to skim a glance over her legs again. They were much, much longer than he had imagined. "It seems I hit closing time. Your assistant said to tell you he'd lock up."

"Oh." Shelby looked over at the windows as if to gauge the time. She never wore a watch when she worked. Using her shoulder, she rubbed at an itch on her cheek. The T-shirt shifted over small, firm breasts. "Well, one of the benefits of owning the place is to open or close when I choose. You can go out and take a look around while I wash up if you'd like."

"Actually..." He gathered the short, tumbling pony-tail into his hand as if testing its weight. "I was thinking more of dinner together. You haven't eaten."

"No, I haven't," Shelby answered, though it hadn't been a question. "But I'm not going out to dinner with you,

Senator. Can I interest you in an Oriental-style crock or a bud vase?"

Alan took a step closer, enjoying her absolute confidence and the idea that he'd be able to shake it. After all, that's why he'd come, wasn't it? he reminded himself. To toss back a few of those clever little potshots she'd taken at his profession, and therefore at him. "We could eat in," he suggested, letting his hand slip from her hair to the back or her neck. "I'm not picky."

"Alan." Shelby gave an exaggerated sigh and pretended there weren't any pulses of pleasure shooting down her spine from the point where his fingers rubbed. "In your profession, you understand policies. Foreign policies, budget policies, defense policies." Unable to resist, she stretched a little under his hand. All the twinges in her muscles had vanished. "I told you mine last night."

"Mmm-hmm." How slender her neck was, he thought. And the skin there was soft enough to give him a hint how she would feel under that apron and T-shirt.

"Well then, there shouldn't be a problem." He must do something physical with his hands, she thought fleetingly. His weren't the palms of a paper-pusher. The edge in her voice was calculated to combat the attraction and the vulnerability that went with it. "You strike me as too intelligent a man to require repetition."

With the slightest pressure, he inched Shelby toward him. "It's standard procedure to review policies from time to time."

"When I do, I'll—" To stop her own forward progress, Shelby pushed a hand against his chest. Both of them remembered the state of her hands at the same time and looked down. Her gurgle of laughter had his eyes lifting back to hers. "You had it coming," she told him, smiling. Her eyes lightened as humor replaced the prickles of tension. His shirt had a fairly clear imprint of her hand, dead center. "This," she said, studying the stain, "might just be the next rage. We should patent it quick. Got any connections?"

"A few." He looked down at his shirt, then back into her face. He didn't mind a bit of dirt when the job called for it. "It'd be an awful lot of paperwork."

"You're right. And since I refuse to fill out any more forms than I already have to, we'd better forget it." Turning away, she began to scrub her hands and arms in a large double sink. "Here, strip that off," she told him as she let the water continue to run. "You'd better get the clay out." Without waiting for an answer, Shelby grabbed a towel and, drying her hands, went to check her kiln.

He wondered, because of the ease of her order, if she made a habit of entertaining half-naked men in her shop. "Did you make everything in the shop?" Alan scanned the shelves after he tugged the shirt over his head. "Everything in here?"

"*Mmm-hmm.*"

"How did you get started?"

"Probably with the modeling clay my governess gave me to keep me out of trouble. I still got into trouble," she added as she checked the vents. "But I really liked poking at the clay. I never had the same feeling for wood or stone." She bent to make an adjustment. Alan turned his head in time to see the denim strain dangerously across her hips. Desire thudded with unexpected force in the pit of his stomach. "How's the shirt?"

Distracted, Alan looked back to where water pounded against cotton. It surprised him that his heartbeat wasn't quite steady. He was going to have to do something about this, he decided. Quite a bit of thinking and reassessing—tomorrow. "It's fine." After switching off the tap, he squeezed the excess water out of the material. "Walking home's going to be...interesting half-dressed," Alan mused as he dropped the shirt over the lip of the sink.

Shelby shot a look over her shoulder, but the retort she had in mind slipped away from her. He was lean enough so she could have counted his ribs, but there was a sense of power and endurance in the breadth of his chest and shoulders, the streamlined waist. His body made her forget any other man she'd ever seen.

It had been he, she realized all at once, whom she'd been thinking of when she'd thrown the clay into that clean-lined bowl.

Shelby let the first flow of arousal rush through her because it was as sweet as it was sharp. Then she tensed against it, rendering it a distant throb she could control.

"You're in excellent shape," she commented lightly. "You should be able to make it to P Street in under three minutes at a steady jog."

"Shelby, that's downright unfriendly."

"I thought is was more rude," she corrected as she struggled against a grin. "I suppose I could be a nice guy and throw it in the dryer for you."

"It was your clay."

"It was *your* move," she reminded him, but snatched up the damp shirt. "Okay, come on upstairs." With one hand, she tugged off her work apron, tossing it aside as she breezed through the doorway. "I suppose you're entitled to one drink on the house."

"You're all heart," Alan murmured as he followed her up the stairs.

"My reputation for generosity precedes me." Shelby pushed open the door. "If you want Scotch, it's over there." Motioning in a vague gesture, she headed in the opposite direction. "If you'd rather have coffee, the kitchen's straight ahead—there's a percolator on the counter and a half-pound in the cabinet next to the window.'' With this, she disappeared with his shirt into an adjoining room.

Alan glanced around. The interest he'd felt for the woman was only increased now by her living quarters. It was a hodgepodge of colors that should have clashed but didn't. Bold greens, vivid blues, and the occasional slash of scarlet. Bohemian. Perhaps flamboyant was a better description. Either adjective fit, just as either fit the woman who lived there. Just as neither fit his life-style or his taste.

There were chunky striped pillows crowded on a long armless sofa. A huge standing urn, deep blue with wild oversize poppies splashed over the surface, held a leafy Roosevelt fern. The rug was a zigzag of color over bare wood.

A wall hanging dominated one side of the room, of a geometric design that gave Alan the impression of a forest fire. A pair of impossibly high Italian heels lay drunkenly next to an ornately carved chair. A mint green ceramic hippopotamus of about three feet in length sat on the other side.

It wasn't a room for quiet contemplation and lazy evenings, but a room of action, energy, and demand.

Alan turned toward the direction Shelby had indicated, then stopped short when he saw the cat. Moshe lay stretched on the arm of a chair, watching him suspiciously out of his good eye. The cat didn't move a whisker, so for a moment Alan took him to be as inanimate as the hippo. The patch should have looked ridiculous, but like the colors in the room, it simply suited.

Above the cat hung an octagon cage. Inside it was a rather drab-looking parrot. Like Moshe, the bird watched

Alan with what seemed to be a mixture of suspicion and curiosity. With a shake of his head for his own fantasies, Alan walked up to them.

"Fix you a drink?" he murmured to the cat, then with an expert's touch he scratched under Moshe's chin. The cat's eyes narrowed with pleasure.

"Well, that shouldn't take more than ten or fifteen minutes," Shelby announced as she came back in. She could hear her cat purring from ten feet away. "So, you've met my roommates."

"Apparently. Why the patch?"

"Moshe Dayan lost his eye in the war. Doesn't like to talk about it." Because her tone seemed too careless for deliberate humor, Alan sent her a searching look she didn't notice as she crossed to the liquor cabinet. "I don't smell any coffee—did you decide on Scotch?"

"I suppose. Does the bird talk?"

"Hasn't said a word in two years." Shelby splashed liquor into glasses. "That's when Moshe came to live with us. Auntie Em's an expert on holding grudges—he only knocked over her cage once."

"Auntie Em?"

"You remember—there's no place like home. Follow the yellow brick road. I've always thought Dorothy's Aunt Em was the quintessential comfortable aunt. Here you go." Walking to him, Shelby offered the glass.

"Thanks." Her choice of names for her pets reminded him that Shelby wasn't altogether the type of woman he thought he'd always understood. "How long have you lived here?"

"*Mmm,* about three years." Shelby dropped onto the couch, drew up her legs, and sat like an Indian. On the coffee table in front of her were a pair of orange-handled scissors, a copy of *The Washington Post* opened to the comic section, a single earring winking with sapphires, what must have been several days worth of unopened mail, and a well-thumbed copy of *Macbeth*.

"I didn't put it together last night," he said as he moved to join her. "Robert Campbell was your father?"

"Yes, did you know him?"

"Of him. I was still in college when he was killed. I've met your mother, of course. She's a lovely woman."

"Yes, she is." Shelby sipped. The Scotch was dark and smooth. "I've often wondered why she never ran for office herself. She's always loved the life.'"

He caught it—the very, very faint edge of resentment. That was something to explore later, Alan decided. Timing was often the ultimate reason for success or failure in any campaign. "You have a brother, don't you?"

"Grant?" For a moment, her gaze touched on the newspaper. "Yes, he steers clear of Washington for the most part." A siren screamed outside the window, echoing then fading. "He prefers the relative peace of Maine." A flicker of amusement crossed her face—a secret that intrigued Alan. Instinct told him he wouldn't learn it yet. Then logic reminded him he had no real interest in her secrets. "In any case, neither of us seem to have inherited the public servant syndrome."

"Is that what you call it?" Alan shifted. The pillow against his back was cool and satin. He imagined her skin would feel like that against his.

"Doesn't it fit?" she countered. "A dedication to the masses, a fetish for paperwork. A taste for power."

It was there again, that light arrogance touched with disdain. "You haven't a taste for power?"

"Just over my own life. I don't like to interfere with other people's."

Alan toyed with the leather thong in her hair until he'd loosened it. Perhaps he had come to debate with her after all. She seemed to urge him to defend what he'd always believed in. "Do you think any of us go through the cycle without touching off ripples in other lives?"

Shelby said nothing as her hair fell free. It tickled her neck, reminding her of the feel of his fingers on almost the same spot. She discovered it was as simple as she had thought it would be to sit beside him with those lean muscles naked and within easy reach.

"It's up to everyone to ward off or work with the ripples in their own way," she said at length. "Well, that does in my philosophy for the day; I'll see if your shirt's dry."

Alan tightened his grip on her hair as she started to rise. Shelby turned her head to find those brooding, considering eyes on her face. "The ripples haven't even started between us," he said quietly. "Perhaps you'd better start working with them."

"Alan..." Shelby kept her voice mild and patient as excitement ripped through her. "I've already told you, *nothing's* going to get started between us. Don't take it personally," she added with a half-smile. "You're very attractive. I'm just not interested."

"No?" With his free hand, he circled her wrist. "Your pulse is racing."

Her annoyance was quick, mirrored in the sudden flare in her eyes, the sudden jerk of her chin. "I'm always happy to boost an ego," she said evenly. "Now, I'll get your shirt."

"Boost it a little higher," he suggested and drew her closer. One kiss, he thought, and he'd be satisfied. Flamboyant, overly aggressive women held no appeal for him. Shelby was certainly that. One kiss, he thought again, and he'd be satisfied on all counts.

She hadn't expected him to be stubborn, any more than she'd expected that fierce tug of longing when his breath fluttered over her lips. She let out a quick sigh of annoyance that she hoped would infuriate him. So, the Senator from Massachusetts wants to try his luck with a free-thinking artist, just for variety. Relaxing, she tilted up her chin. All right, then, she decided. She'd give him a kiss that would knock him flat—right before she bundled him up and hauled him out the door.

But he didn't touch his lips to hers yet, only looked at her. Why wasn't she handling him? she wondered as his mouth slowly lowered. Why wasn't she...? Then his tongue traced a lazy line over her lips and she wasn't capable of wondering. There was nothing more she could do other than close her eyes and experience.

She'd never known anyone to take such care with a kiss—and his lips had yet to touch hers. The tip of his tongue outlined and tested the fullness of her mouth so softly, so slowly. All sensation, all arousal, was centered there. How could she have known a mouth could feel so much? How could she have known a kiss that wasn't a kiss would make her incapable of moving?

Then he captured her bottom lip between his teeth and her breath started to shudder. He nibbled, then drew it inside his mouth to suck until she felt the answering, unrelenting tug deep inside her. There was a rhythm, he was guiding her to it, and Shelby had forgotten to resist. His thumb was running up then down over the vein in her wrist; his fingertips skimmed the base of her neck. The points of pleasure spread out until her whole body hummed with them. Still his lips hadn't pressed onto her.

She moaned, a low, throaty sound that was as much of demand as surrender. Then they were mouth to mouth, spinning from arousal to passion at the instant of contact.

He'd known her mouth would taste like this—hot and eager. He'd known her body would be like this against his—soft and strong. Had that been why he'd woken thinking of her? Had that been why he'd found himself standing outside her shop as afternoon was waning into evening? For the first time in his life, Alan found that the reasons didn't matter. They were pressed close, and that was enough for him.

Her hair carried that undefinable scent he remembered. He dove his hands into it as if he would have the fragrance seep into his pores. It drove him deeper. Her tongue met his, seeking, searching, until her taste was all the tastes he'd ever coveted. The pillows rustled with soft whispers as he pressed her between them and himself.

She hadn't expected this kind of raw, consuming passion from him. Style—she would have expected style and a seduction with all the traditional trimmings. Those she could have resisted or evaded. But there was no resisting a need that had so quickly found and tapped her own. There was no evading a passion that had already captured her. She ran her hands up his naked back and moaned as the feel of him lit new fires.

This was something too firm to be molded, too hard to be changed. The man had styled himself as he had chosen. Shelby knew it instinctively and felt desire rise for this reason alone. But with desire came the knowledge that she was growing too soft, too pliant; came the fear that he might have already changed her shape with a kiss.

"Alan." She gathered her forces for resistance when every pore, every cell, was crying out for her to submit. "Enough," she managed against his mouth.

"Not nearly," he corrected, trapping her close when she would have struggled away.

He was taking her deep again, where she had no control over the moment, or the outcome of it.

"Alan." She drew back far enough to see his face. "I want you to stop." Her breathing wasn't steady, her eyes were dark as smoke, but the resistance in her body was very real. Alan felt a hot flash of anger, which he expertly controlled, and a sharp stab of desire, which he had more trouble with.

"All right." He loosened his hold. "Why?"

It was rare for her to have to order herself to do something as natural as relax. Even after she had, there was a light band of tension at the base of her neck. "You kiss very well," she said with forced casualness.

"For a politician?"

Shelby let out a little hiss of breath and rose. Damn him for knowing just what rib to punch—and for his skill in punching without raising a sweat. Pompous, Shelby told herself. Pompous, smug, and self-absorbed.

The apartment was nearly dark. She flicked on a light, surprised that so much time had passed when everything had seemed to happen so quickly. "Alan..." Shelby linked her hands together as she did when she'd decided to be patient.

"You didn't answer my question," he pointed out and made himself relax against the pillows that brought back memories of her skin.

"Perhaps I haven't made myself clear enough." She fought the urge to say something that would erase that mildly interested look in his eyes. Damn, he was clever, she thought grudgingly—with words, with expressions. She'd like to come up against him again when her heart wasn't thudding. "I meant everything I said last night."

"So did I." He tilted his head as if to study her from a new angle. "But maybe like your bird, you're quite an expert on holding grudges too."

When she stiffened, the hands that were linked fell apart. "Don't press."

"I generally don't on old wounds." The hurt was there; he saw it, and an anger that was well rooted. It was difficult for him to remember he'd known her for less than a day and had no right to pry, or to expect. "I'm sorry," he added as he rose.

Her rigidness vanished with the apology. He had a way of saying simple things with simple genuineness, Shelby thought, and found she liked him for it—if for nothing else. "It's all right." She crossed the room and came back moments later with his shirt. "Good as new," she promised as she tossed it to him. "Well, it's been nice; don't let me keep you."

He had to grin. "Am I being helped out the door?"

Not bothering to disguise a smile, she gave a mock sigh. "I've always been too obvious. Good night, Senator. Look both ways when you cross the street." She went to open the side door that led to the outside stairs.

Alan pulled the shirt over his head before he crossed to her. He'd always thought it had been his brother, Caine, who'd never been able to take a simple no with a polite bow. Perhaps he'd been wrong, Alan mused, and it was a basic MacGregor trait. "The Scotch can be stubborn," he commented as he paused beside her.

"You'll remember I'm a Campbell. Who'd know better?" Shelby opened the door a bit wider.

"Then, we both know where we stand." He cupped her chin in his hand to hold her face still as he gave her a last hard kiss that seemed suspiciously like a threat. "Till next time."

Shelby closed the door behind him and stood leaning against it a moment. He was going to be trouble, she decided. Alan MacGregor was going to be very serious trouble.

Chapter Three

It turned out to be busy for a Monday morning. By eleven, Shelby had sold several pieces, including three that she had taken out of the kiln only the evening before. Between customers, she sat behind the counter wiring a lamp she had made in the shape of a Greek amphora. To have simply sat during the idle time would have been impossible for her. To have dusted or fiddled with the displays would have bored her to distraction. She left such things to Kyle, to their mutual satisfaction.

Because it was warm, she kept the door of the shop open. It was, Shelby knew, more tempting to stroll through an open door than to open a closed one. Spring came in, along with the unique sound of cars riding over cobblestone. She had a steady stream of browsers who bought nothing. Shelby didn't mind. They were company as much as potential buyers. The woman carrying the manicured poodle in a hand-knit sweater was an interesting diversion. The restless teenager who came in to poke around gave her a chance to touch on the problems of youth and unemployment. Shelby hired him to wash the windows. While she wired, the boy stood on the street side running a squeegee over the glass while a portable radio bounced out tunes at his feet. She enjoyed the sound as it mixed with the occasional snatches of conversations from passersby.

Did you see the price of that dress?
If he doesn't call me tonight, I'm going to...
...notes on her lecture on pre-Hitler Germany.

Idly she finished the conversations in her head as she worked. Shelby was threading the wire up the inside of the lamp when Myra Ditmeyer sauntered in. She wore a breezy vermilion suit that matched the shade of her lipstick. The powerful punch of her scent filled the little shop.

"Well, Shelby, always keeping those clever hands busy."

With a smile of pure pleasure, Shelby leaned over the counter to kiss Myra's powdered cheek. If you want some acerbic gossip or just plain fun, there was no one, in Shelby's opinion, better than Myra. "I thought you'd be home planning all the wonderful things you're going to feed me tonight."

"Oh, my dear, that's all seen to." Myra set down her alligator bag. "The cook's in a creative spin even as we speak."

"I've always loved eating at your house." Shelby pulled the wire through the top of the lamp. "None of those stingy little meals or inedible sauces disguised as exotic." Absently she tapped her foot to the beat of the radio. "You did say Mama was coming."

"Yes, with Ambassador Dilleneau."

"Oh, yeah—the Frenchman with the big ears."

"Is that any way to talk about a diplomat?"

"She's been seeing him quite a bit," Shelby said casually. "I've wondered if I'm going to have a Gallic step-papa."

"You could do worse," Myra pointed out.

"*Mmm.* So, tell me, Myra..." Shelby attached the light fixture to the cord with a few deft turns. "Who've you set up for me tonight?"

"Set up," Myra repeated, wrinkling her nose. "What an unromantic phrase."

"Sorry. How about—who are you planning to loose Cupid's arrows on?"

"It's still unromantic when you're smirking." Myra watched Shelby screw in a light bulb. "In any case, I think you should be surprised. You've always been fond of surprises."

"I like giving better than getting."

"How well I know. How old were you? Eight, as I recall, when you and Grant... surprised a small, rather influential gathering in your mother's parlor with uncomfortably accurate caricatures of the Cabinet."

"It was Grant's idea," Shelby said, with a lingering twinge of regret that she hadn't thought of it first. "Papa laughed about it for days."

"He had a unique sense of humor."

"As *I* recall you offered Grant two thousand for the one of the Secretary of State."

"And the scoundrel wouldn't sell it to me. Good God," she mused. "What it would be worth now?"

"It would depend what name he signed to it, wouldn't it?"

"How is Grant? I haven't seen him since Christmas."

"The same—brilliant, grumpy." A laugh stole through the words. "Guarding his lighthouse fortress and his anonymity. I think I might sneak up there and bother him for a couple of weeks this summer."

"Such a gorgeous young man," Myra mused. "What a waste for him to seclude himself on that little bit of coast."

"It's what he wants," Shelby said simply. "For now."

"Excuse me?"

Both women looked toward the door where a young man stood in a crisp messenger's uniform. Shelby glanced at the basket over his arm. "Can I help you?"

"Miss Shelby Campbell?"

"Yes, I'm Shelby."

He shifted the basket he carried from his arm to his hand as he walked to her. "Delivery for you, Miss Campbell."

"Thanks." Automatically, she reached into the cash drawer for a dollar. "Who's it from?"

"Card's inside," he told her, pocketing the bill. "Enjoy."

She played the game. Shelby had been known to study and poke at a package on Christmas morning for twenty minutes before ripping off the paper. There were such possibilities in the unknown. She tilted the package from side to side, peered at it, then cupped her chin on both hands and stared at it.

"Oh, come on, Shelby!" Myra shifted her weight from foot to foot with impatience. "Lift off the cover; I'm dying to see."

"In a minute," Shelby murmured. "It might be—a picnic. Who'd send me a picnic? Or a puppy." She bent her ear close and listened. "Too quiet for a puppy. And it smells like . . ." Closing her eyes she drew in a deep breath and held it. "That's funny, who'd send me—" She opened the lid. "Strawberries."

The basket was rich with them—plump and moistly red. Their scent drifted up with memories of the sun-warmed field they'd been plucked from. Shelby lifted one and held it under her nose, savoring.

"Wonderful," she decided. "Really, really wonderful.

Myra plucked one out and bit it neatly in half. *"Mmm."* She popped the rest into her mouth. "Aren't you going to read the card?"

Still holding the berry, Shelby lifted out the plain white envelope, balancing it in her palm as if testing the weight. She turned it over, held it up to the light then turned it back to the front.

"Shelby!"

"Oh, all right." She ripped open the seal and drew out the card.

Shelby,
They made me think of you.

Alan

Watching her carefully, Myra saw the surprise, the pleasure, and something that wasn't regret or wariness but had aspects of both.

"Anyone I know?" she said dryly when Shelby didn't speak.

"What?" She looked up blankly, then shook her head. "Yes, I suppose you do." But she slipped the card back into the envelope without saying. "Myra." The name was on a long drawn-out sigh. "I think I'm in trouble."

"Good." She gave Shelby a smug smile and a nod. "It's about time you were. Would you like me to drive my cook crazy and add another name to my list for dinner tonight?"

Oh, it was tempting. Shelby nearly agreed before she stopped herself. "No. No, I don't think it would be wise."

"Only the young think they know anything about wisdom," Myra stated with a sniff. "Very well, then; I'll see you at seven." She chose another berry before she picked up her purse. "Oh, and Shelby, pack up that lamp and bring it along. Just put it on my account."

She'd have to call him, Shelby told herself when she was alone. Dammit, she'd have to call and thank him. She bit into a berry so that the juice and sweetness exploded inside her mouth—a sensual taste, part sun, part earth. And she remembered how Alan's taste had exploded inside her mouth.

Why hadn't he sent her something ordinary like flowers? Flowers she could have passed off and forgotten. She looked down into the basket, filled with berries brilliantly red and begging to be tasted. How did you deal with a man who sent you a basket of strawberries on a spring morning?

He'd known it, of course, she decided abruptly. A man like him would be a quick and clever judge of people. She felt simultaneous twinges of annoyance and admiration. She didn't like to be read so easily but...she couldn't help respecting someone who could.

Leaving the lid open, Shelby reached for the phone.

Alan calculated he had between fifteen and twenty minutes before the Senate was called back to the floor. He'd use the time to review the proposed budget cuts. A deficit that edged uncomfortably close to two-hundred billion had to be trimmed, but Alan viewed the proposed cuts in education as unacceptable. Congress had already partially rejected the sought-after domestic spending cuts, and he felt he had enough support to influence a modification on the education snipping.

There was more on his mind than deficits and budgets, however. Though it was the spring following an election year, Alan had been approached by the Senate Majority Leader. He'd been carefully felt out by an expert at saying nothing while hardly pausing for breath. It didn't take magic for Alan to conclude that he was being considered as the party's hope for the next decade. But did he want the top rung?

He'd thought about it—he wasn't a fool or without ambition. Still, he had believed if he ever decided to take a grab at the presidential brass ring, it would be in another fifteen, perhaps twenty years. The possibility of making his move sooner, at his party's urging, was something he would have to weigh carefully.

Nevertheless, as far as Alan's father was concerned, there had never been any question that his eldest son would run for president—and win. Daniel MacGregor liked to think he still held the strings guiding his offsprings' lives. Sometimes they gave him the gift of his illusions. Alan could still remember his sister's announcement of her pregnancy that past winter. Daniel's attention was centered on that and the marriage of their brother, Caine, so that the pressure had lifted from Alan. For now, he thought wryly. It shouldn't be long before he got one of his father's famous phone calls.

Your mother misses you. She worries about you. When are you going to take the time to come visit? Why aren't you married yet? Your sister can't carry on the line by herself, you know.

That might be simplifying it, Alan thought with a grin. But that would be the essence of the call. Strange, he'd always been able to shrug off his father's views on marriage and children. But now...

Why was it a woman he'd met only a few days before made him think of marriage? People didn't bind themselves willingly to someone they didn't know. She wasn't even the type of woman who'd appealed to him in the past. She wasn't sleek and cool. She wouldn't be undemanding, or make a comfortable hostess for elegant state dinners. She wouldn't be gracious, and she'd be anything but tactful. And, Alan added with a glimmer of a smile, she wouldn't even have dinner with him.

A challenge. She would be a challenge and he'd always enjoyed working his way through one. But that wasn't why. A mystery. She was a mystery and he'd always liked solving them, step by step. But that wasn't why. She had the verve of the very young, the skill of an artist and the flash of a rebel. She had passion that boiled rather than simmered and eyes as quiet as a foggy evening. She had a child's mouth and a woman's allure and a mind that would never adhere to the logical one-step-at-a-time structure of his own. The chemistry between them was almost absurdly wrong. And yet . . .

And yet, at thirty-five, Alan suddenly believed there was such a phenomenon as love at first sight. So, he would wage his patience and tenacity against her flash and energy and see who won in the end. If indeed there could ever be a winner between oil and water.

The phone rang beside him. Alan let it go until he remembered his secretary wasn't in the outer office. Mildly annoyed, he pushed the blinking button and answered. "Senator MacGregor."

"Thanks."

His lips curved as he leaned back in his chair. "You're welcome. How do they taste?"

Shelby brought a berry to her mouth for a nibble. "Fantastic. My shop smells like a strawberry patch. Dammit, Alan," she said with an exasperated sigh. "Strawberries are an unfair tactic. You're supposed to fight with orchids or diamonds. I could have coped very nicely with a big tacky diamond or five-dozen African orchids."

He tapped the pen he'd been using on the stack of papers on his desk. "I'll be certain not to give you either. When are you going to see me, Shelby?"

She was silent for a moment, torn, tempted. Ridiculous, she thought, shaking her head. Just because he had a bit of whimsy under the political protocol was no reason to toss aside a lifelong belief. "Alan, it simply wouldn't work. I'm saving us both a lot of trouble by saying no."

"You don't strike me as the type to avoid trouble."

"Maybe not—I'm making an exception in your case. Years from now, when you have ten grandchildren and bursitis, you'll thank me."

"Do I have to wait that long for you to have dinner with me?"

She laughed, cursing him at the same time. "I really like you." He heard another quick sound of frustration. "Dammit, Alan, don't be charming anymore. We'll both end up on thin ice. I just can't take it breaking under me again."

He started to speak, then heard the signal—the buzzers and lights that warned of a quorum call. "Shelby, I have to go. We're going to talk about this some more."

"No." Her voice was firm now as she cursed herself for saying more than she had intended. "I hate repeating myself. It's boring. Just consider that I've done you a favor. Good-bye, Alan."

She hung up, then slammed the lid closed on the strawberries. Oh, God, she asked herself, how had he managed to get to her so quickly?

While she dressed for Myra's dinner party, Shelby listened to an old Bogart film. She listened only because the television had lost its shaky grip on the horizontal hold two weeks before. Currently she was amused by the situation.

It was like having a large, rather ostentatious radio that took a great deal more imagination than a full-color twenty-inch screen.

While Bogey spoke in his weary, tough-guy voice, she slipped her narrow beaded vest over her frilled lace shirt.

Shelby had shoved aside her uncertain mood of the afternoon. She had always believed if you simply refused to admit you were upset or to acknowledge depression, you wouldn't be upset or depressed. In any case, she was sure that now that she had made herself crystal-clear and had refused Alan MacGregor for the third time, he would get the picture.

If she regretted the fact that there would be no more baskets of strawberries or surprises, she told herself she didn't. No one could make Shelby believe that something that she said was untrue was really more true than Shelby would admit to herself.

She stepped into a pair of foolish evening shoes that had more heel than leather as she dropped a few essentials into her bag—keys, a well-used lipstick and a half-roll of Life Savers.

"Are you staying in tonight, Moshe?" she asked as she passed by the cat who lounged on her bed. When he only opened his eye in acknowledgment, she breezed out of the room. "Okay, don't wait up." Shelby dropped her purse on top of the box that held Myra's lamp and prepared to lift both when someone knocked on the door. "You expecting someone?" she asked Auntie Em. The bird merely fluttered her wings, unconcerned. Hefting the box, Shelby went to answer.

Pleasure. She had to acknowledge it as well as annoyance when she saw Alan. "Another neighborly visit?" she asked, planting herself in the doorway. She skimmed a glance down the silk tie and trim, dark suit. "You don't look dressed for strolling."

The sarcasm didn't concern him—he'd seen that quick flash of unguarded pleasure. "As a public servant, I feel an obligation to conserve our natural resources and protect the environment." Reaching over, he clipped a tiny sprig of sweet pea into her hair. "I'm going to give you a lift to the Ditmeyers'. You might say we're carpooling."

Shelby could smell the fragrance that drifted from just above her right ear. She had an urge to put her hand up and feel the small blossoms. Since when, she demanded of herself, had she been so vulnerable to charm? "You're going to Myra's little . . . get-together?"

"Yes. Are you ready?"

Shelby narrowed her eyes, trying to figure out how Myra could have learned the name of the strawberry sender. "When did she ask you?"

"Hmm?" He was distracted by the way the thin lace rose at her neck. "Last week—at the Writes'."

Some of her suspicions eased. Perhaps it was just coincidence after all. "Well, I appreciate the offer, Senator, but I'll drive myself. See you over the canapés."

"Then, I'll ride with you," he said amiably. "We don't want to put any more carbon monoxide in the air than necessary. Shall I put that in the car for you?"

Shelby took a firmer grip on the box as her hold in other areas started to slip. It was that damn serious smile and those thoughtful eyes, she decided. They made a woman feel as though she were the only one he'd ever looked at in quite that way.

"Alan," she began, a bit amused by his persistence. "What is this?"

"This . . ." He leaned over and captured her mouth with his, lingering until her fingers threatened to dig holes in the stiff cardboard she held. "Is what our ancestors would have called a siege," he finished softly. "And Mac-Gregors are notoriously successful at laying siege."

Her breath shuddered out to merge with his. "You don't do badly at hand-to-hand combat either." He chuckled and would have kissed her again if she hadn't managed to step back. "All right." Shelby thrust the box into his arms, considering it a strategic move. "We'll carpool. I don't want to be condemned as an air-polluter. You drive," she decided with a sudden mood-switching grin. "Then, I can have an extra glass of wine at dinner."

"You left your TV on," Alan commended as he stepped aside to let her pass.

"That's all right. It's broken anyway." Shelby clattered down the steps, heedless of her fragile heels and the steep drop. The sun had nearly set, sending wild streaks of red into a darkening, sober sky. Shelby laughed, turning back to Alan when she reached the narrow alleyway. "Carpool, my foot. But it's still not a date, MacGregor. What we'll call this is a . . . a civilized transit agreement. That sounds bureaucratic enough. I like your car," she added, patting the hood of his Mercedes. "Very sedate."

Alan opened the trunk and set the box inside. He glanced back up at Shelby as he closed it. "You have an interesting way of insulting someone."

She laughed, that free smoke-edged laugh as she went to him. "Dammit, Alan, I like you." Throwing her arms around his neck, she gave him a friendly hug that sent jolts of need careening through him. "I really like you," she added, tilting back her head with a smile that lit her whole face with a sense of fun. "I could probably have said that to a dozen other men who'd never have realized I was insulting them."

"So." His hands settled at her hips. "I get points for perception."

"And a few other things." When her gaze slipped to his mouth, she felt the strength of longing weaken all the memories and all the vows. "I'm going to hate myself for this," she murmured. "But I want to kiss you again. Here, while the light's fading." Her eyes came back to his, still smiling, but darkened with an anticipation he knew had nothing to do with surrender. "I've always thought you could do mad things at dusk without any consequences."

Tightening her arms around his neck, Shelby pressed her mouth to his.

He was careful, very careful not to give in to the urgent desire to drag her closer. This time he'd let her lead him, and in doing so, lead herself where he wanted them both to go.

The light was softly dying. There was an impatient honking from the street on the other side of the shop. Through the window of the apartment across the alley came the rich tang of spaghetti sauce and the bluesy sounds of an old Gershwin record. Straining closer, Shelby felt the fast, even beat of Alan's heart against her own.

His taste was the same quietly debilitating flavor as she remembered. Shelby could hardly believe she'd lived for so long without knowing that one particular taste. It seemed less possible she'd be able to live without it now. Or the feel of those strong steady arms around her—the firm body that transmitted safety and danger to her at the same time.

He'd know how to protect her if something threatened. He knew how to take her to the brink of an abyss she'd so cleverly avoided. And Shelby was too aware that he could take her over the edge.

But his mouth was so tempting, his taste so enticing. And dusk was still holding back the night sky. She gave herself to it longer than she should have—and not as long as she wanted to.

"Alan..." He felt his name form against his lips before she drew away. Their gaze held a moment while his arms and hers kept their bodies pressed close. There was strength in his face—a face she could trust. But there was so much between them. "We'd better go," Shelby murmured. "It's nearly dark."

The Ditmeyers' home was lit though there was still color in the western sky. Shelby could just see the riot of phlox in the rock garden as she stepped from the car. Her mother was already there, Shelby discovered when she caught a glimpse of the diplomatic plates on the Lincoln in the drive.

"You know Ambassador Dilleneau?" Shelby offered her hand to Alan as they stepped onto the walk.

"Slightly."

"He's in love with my mother." She brushed her bangs out of her eyes as she turned to him. "Men are, typically, but I think she has a soft spot for him."

"That amuses you?" Watching her, Alan pressed the doorbell.

"A little," she admitted. "It's rather sweet. She blushes," Shelby added with a quick laugh. "It's a very odd feeling for a daughter to see her mother blush over a man."

"You wouldn't?" Alan skimmed a thumb over her cheekbone. Shelby forgot her mother altogether.

"Wouldn't what?"

"Blush," he said softly, tracing her jawline. "Over a man."

"Once—I was twelve and he was thirty-two." She had to talk—just keep talking to remember who she was. "He, uh, came to fix the water heater."

"How'd he make you blush?"

"He grinned at me. He had a chipped tooth I thought was really sexy."

On a quick ripple of laughter, Alan kissed her just as Myra opened the door.

"Well, well." She didn't bother to disguise a self-satisfied smile. "Good evening. I see you two have met."

"What makes you think that?" Shelby countered breezily as she stepped inside.

Myra glanced from one to the other. "Do I smell strawberries?" she asked sweetly.

"Your lamp." Shelby gave her a bland look and indicated the box Alan carried. "Where would you like it?"

"Oh, just set it down there, Alan. It's so nice to have just a few friends in," Myra continued as she tucked an arm through each of theirs. "Gossip is so much more intimate that way. Herbert, pour two more of those marvelous aperitifs—you must try it," she added to both Shelby and Alan. "I've just discovered this marvelous little blackberry liqueur."

"Herbert." Shelby walked over to the Justice and gave him a smacking kiss. "You've been out sailing again." She grinned at his sunburned nose. "When are we going to the beach to wind-surf?"

"The child almost makes me believe I could do it," he commented as he gave her a squeeze. "Good to see you, Alan." His face folded into comfortable grandfatherly lines that made people forget he was one of the top judiciary figures in the country. "I think you know everyone. I'll just get those drinks."

"Hello, Mama." Shelby bent to kiss her mother's cheek when the emerald clusters on Deborah's ears caught her eye. "I haven't seen these before—I'd have borrowed them immediately."

"Anton gave them to me." A delicate color seeped into her cheeks. "In—appreciation for that party I hostessed for him."

"I see." Shelby's gaze shifted to the trim Frenchman beside her mother. "You have exquisite taste, Ambassador," she told him as she offered her hand.

His eyes twinkled as he brought it to his lips—a trait that made up for the ears as far as Shelby was concerned. "You look lovely as always, Shelby. Senator, a pleasure to see you in such a relaxed atmosphere."

"Senator MacGregor." Deborah smiled up at him. "I didn't realize you and Shelby were acquainted."

"We're working on disrupting an old family tradition." He accepted the glass the Justice offered.

"He means feud," Shelby explained at her mother's blank look. She sipped the liqueur, approved it, then sat on the arm of Myra's chair.

"Oh... *Oh*," Deborah repeated as she remembered. "The Campbells and the MacGregors were blood enemies in Scotland—though I can't quite remember why."

"They stole our land," Alan put in mildly.

"That's what you say." Shelby shot him a look as she sipped again. "We *acquired* MacGregor land through a royal decree. They weren't good sports about it."

Alan gave her a thoughtful smile. "I'd be interested to hear you debate that issue with my father."

"What a match," Myra said, brightening at the thought. "Herbert, can you just see our Shelby nose-to-nose with Daniel? All that red hair and stubbornness. You really should arrange it, Alan."

"I've been giving it some thought."

"Have you?" Shelby's brows lifted to disappear completely under her frizz of bangs.

"Quite a bit of thought," he said in the same even tone.

"I've been to that wonderful anachronism in Hyannis Port." Myra gave Shelby a brief pat on the thigh. "It's right up your alley, dear. She's so fond of the—well, let's say unique, shall we?"

"Yes." Deborah sent Shelby a fond smile. "I could never figure out why. But then, both of my children have always been a mystery. Perhaps it's because they're so bright and clever and restless. I'm always hoping they'll settle down." This time she beamed the smile at Alan. "You're not married either, are you, Senator?"

"If you'd like," Shelby said as she studied the color of her liqueur through the crystal, "I could just step out while you discuss the terms of the dowry."

"Shelby, really," Deborah murmured over the sound of the Justice's chuckle.

"It's so difficult for parents to see their children as capable adults," the Ambassador commented in his light, soothing voice. "For myself, I have two daughters with children of their own. Still, I worry. How are your children, Myra? You have a new grandson, don't you?"

Nothing could have been better calculated to change the subject. Shelby sent him a faint admiring nod and watched his eyes twinkle as Myra began an enthusiastic description of her grandson's first tooth.

He'd suit her, Shelby decided, watching her mother from under her lashes. She was the type of woman who never felt quite whole without a man. And she'd been shaped and polished into a political wife years before. The gloss was still there. Elegant manners, elegant style, elegant patience. Shelby gave a little sigh she didn't even hear.

How could she and her mother look so much alike and be so very different? Elegance had always seemed a silk-lined cage to Shelby—and a cage equaled restrictions no matter how it was formed. She still remembered too many of them.

The bodyguards—discreet, but always there. The carefully screened parties, the sophisticated alarm systems, the intrusion of the press. The security hadn't saved her father, though a photographer had gotten an award-winning picture of the gunman—seconds too late to do any good.

Shelby knew what was behind the elegance; the state dinners, the speeches, the galas. There were a hundred tiny fears, a millennium of doubts. The memory of too many political assassinations and assassination attempts in hardly more than twenty years.

No, her mother was made for the life. Patient, with a rod of steel beneath the fragile skin. Shelby wouldn't choose it, nor would she let it choose her. She'd love no one who could leave her again so horribly.

Letting the conversation flow around her, Shelby tilted back her glass. Her eyes met Alan's. It was there—that quietly brooding patience that promised to last a lifetime. She could almost feel him calmly peeling off layer after layer of whatever bits and pieces made up her personality to get to the tiny core she kept private.

You bastard. She nearly said it out loud. Certainly it reflected in her eyes for he smiled at her in simple acknowledgment. The siege was definitely under way. She only hoped she had enough provisions to outlast him.

Chapter Four

Shelby put in a very full week, dominated by the creative overload she experienced every few months. Kyle managed the shop for three days running while she closeted herself in her workroom, to sit for hours at the wheel or with her glazes. If she started at 7:00 A.M., Shelby still had enough juice to toss clay until late into the night. She knew herself well enough to understand and to accept that this sort of mood struck her when she was having trouble blocking out something that worried her.

When she worked, she would focus both mind and emotion on the project in her hands, and in that way, whatever problem she had simply ceased to be a problem for that amount of time. Normally when she'd run out of steam, she'd come up with a solution. Not this time.

The impetus that had driven her most of the week dried up late Friday night. Alan was still lodged in her mind. He shouldn't have been. Shelby could tell herself that as impatiently as she liked, but it didn't change the fact that he was as firmly in her thoughts as he had been when they'd last been together.

It hadn't mattered that she'd managed to keep the rest of the evening at the Ditmeyers' casual. Alan had still stopped her in her tracks with one of those slow, devastating kisses at her side door. He hadn't insisted on coming in. Shelby might have been grateful for that if she hadn't suspected it was just part of his planned siege. Confuse the enemy, assail her with doubts, leave her with her nerve ends tingling. Very clever strategy.

He'd been in Boston for several days—Shelby knew because he'd called to tell her he was going, though she'd given him no encouragement. She told herself it was a respite. If he was a few hundred miles away, he couldn't be popping up on her doorstep unexpectedly. She told herself when and if he popped up again, she'd keep the door locked. She wanted badly to believe she could.

Then halfway through the week the pig had come—a big lavender stuffed pig with a foolish grin and velvet ears. Shelby had tried to toss it into a closet and forget it. He seemed to know that the way to get to her was through her sense of the ridiculous. She hadn't thought he had one—he shouldn't have, but there it was. What was a man who had such stuffy, straight-line views on rules and order doing buying stuffed animals anyway? She'd nearly softened. It was nice to know he was capable of such a gesture, particularly since it was so out of character. It was nice to know that she was the one who brought out that side of him. But... There was no way Alan was going to weaken her resolve with a silly toy that was meant for children or softheaded women.

She called it MacGregor and kept it on her bed—a joke on both of them, she thought. The pig was the only MacGregor she was going to sleep with.

But she dreamed of him. At night, in her big brass bed, no matter how hard she had worked, no matter how many friends she had been with, it always came back to Alan. Once she imagined there were a dozen of him, surrounding her town house. She couldn't go out without being captured; she couldn't stay in without going mad. She woke cursing him and his sieges and her own fertile imagination.

By the end of the week, Shelby promised herself she wouldn't accept any more deliveries and would simply hang up when she heard Alan's voice on the phone. If reason and patience hadn't gotten through to him, downright rudeness would. Even a MacGregor had to have some common sense.

Because of the schedule she'd put herself on the week before, Shelby had given Kyle the keys to the shop with instructions that he open up at ten on Saturday. She was sleeping in. There wasn't any need to go into her workroom, even if some of the creative juices had still been flowing. In the past few days, she had accumulated enough inventory to last for weeks. Now she would put as much thought and energy into being lazy as she had put into slaving.

Shelby heard the knock on the door, and shifting under the sheets, considered ignoring it. Still half-asleep, she tumbled out of bed. It simply wasn't in her makeup to let a ringing phone or a knock go unanswered. Because she tripped over the robe she'd thrown on the floor the night before, Shelby remembered to tug it on as she walked from the room. With her eyes narrowed protectively against the sunlight, she opened the door.

"'Morning, Miss Campbell. Another delivery."

The boy who had brought her both the strawberries and the pig stood in the doorway and grinned.

"Thanks." Too disoriented to remember her vow, Shelby reached out. He handed her the bound-together strings of two-dozen pink and yellow balloons. He was gone and Shelby was back inside before she woke up enough to realize what had happened. "Oh, no." Looking up, she watched the balloons dance at the tops of their strings. Hanging by a ribbon at the end was a little white card.

She wouldn't even open it, she told herself. She knew who they were from anyway. Who else? No, she wasn't going to open it. In fact, she was going to find a pin and pop every last balloon. What were they but a bunch of hot air? It was ridiculous. To prove a point, Shelby let the strings go so the balloons drifted up to the ceiling. If he thought he was going to win her over with silly presents and clever little notes . . . he was absolutely right, dammit.

Shelby jumped up, swearing when she missed the strings by inches. Hauling over a chair, she climbed into it and grabbed the card.

The yellow's for sunshine, the pink's for spring. Share them with me.

Alan

"You drive me crazy," she muttered, standing in the chair with the balloons in one hand and the card in the other. How did he know, how *could* he know just the sort of thing that would get to her? Strawberries and pigs and balloons—it was hopeless. Shelby stared up at them, wishing she didn't need to smile.

It was time to be firm—very, very firm, she told herself as she stepped down. If she ignored it, he'd just send her something else. So, she'd call him and tell him—no, she'd *demand* that he stop. She'd say he was annoying—no, *boring* her. Boring was unforgivably insulting. Shelby twisted the balloon strings around her wrist as she reached for the phone. He'd given her his home number, which she'd refused to write down. Of course, she remembered every digit. As she pushed buttons Shelby worked herself into her haughtiest mood.

"Hello."

Her mood deflated as if she'd been pricked with a pin. "Alan."

"Shelby."

She struggled not to be moved by the quiet, serious tone that should never have moved her. She liked men with a laugh in their voice. "Alan, this has to stop."

"Does is? It hasn't even started."

"Alan—" She tried to remember her decision to be firm. "I mean it. You have to stop sending me things; you're only wasting your time."

"I have a bit to spare," he said mildly. "How was your week?"

"Busy. Listen, I—"

"I missed you."

The simple statement threw the rest of her lecture into oblivion. "Alan, don't—"

"Every day," he continued. "Every night. Have you been to Boston, Shelby?"

"Uh . . . yes," she managed, busy fighting off the weakness creeping into her. Helplessly she stared up at the balloons. How could she fight something so insubstantial it floated?

"I'd like to take you there in the fall, when it smells of damp leaves and smoke."

Shelby told herself her heart was not fluttering. "Alan, I didn't call to talk about Boston. Now, to put it in very simple terms, I want you to stop calling me, I want you to stop dropping by, and—" Her voice began to rise in frustration as she pictured him listening with that patient, serious smile and calm eyes. "I want you to stop sending me balloons and pigs and everything! Is that clear?"

"Perfectly. Spend the day with me."

Did the man never stop being patient? She couldn't abide patient men. "For God's sake, Alan!"

"We'll call it an experimental outing," he suggested in the same even tone. "Not a date."

"No!" she said, barely choking back a laugh. Couldn't abide it, she tried to remember. She preferred the flashy, the freewheeling. "No, no, no!"

"Not bureaucratic enough." His voice was so calm, so…so *senatorial*, she decided, she wanted to scream. But the scream bubbled perilously close to another laugh. "All right, let me think—a standard daytime expedition for furthering amiable relations between opposing clans."

"You're trying to be charming again," Shelby muttered.

"Am I succeeding?"

Some questions were best ignored. "I really don't know how to be more succinct, Alan."

Was that part of the appeal? he wondered. The fact that the free-spirited Gypsy could turn into the regal duchess in the blink of an eye. He doubted she had any notion she was as much one as the other. "You have a wonderful speaking voice. What time will you be ready?"

Shelby huffed and frowned and considered. "*If* I agree to spend some time with you today, will you stop sending me things?"

Alan was silent for a long moment. "Are you going to take a politician's word?"

Now she had to laugh. "All right, you've boxed me in on that one."

"It's a beautiful day, Shelby. I haven't had a free Saturday in over a month. Come out with me."

She twined the phone cord around her finger. A refusal seemed so petty, so bad-natured. He was really asking her for very little, and—dammit—she wanted to see him. "All right, Alan, every rule needs to be bent a bit now and again to prove it's really a rule after all."

"If you say so. Where would you like to go? There's an exhibition of Flemish art at the National Gallery."

Shelby's lips curved. "The zoo," she said and waited for his reaction.

"Fine," Alan agreed without missing a beat. "I'll be there in ten minutes."

With a sigh, Shelby decided he just wasn't an easy man to shake. "Alan, I'm not dressed."

"I'll be there in five."

On a burst of laughter, she slammed down the phone.

"I like the snakes. They're so slimily arrogant."

While Alan watched, Shelby pressed close to the glass to study a boa who looked more bored than disdainful. When she had suggested the zoo, he hadn't been certain if she had done so because she wanted to go or had wanted to see how he would react. It didn't take a great deal of thought to discern it had been a combination of both.

A visit to the National Zoo on a sunny spring Saturday promised crowds and hordes of children. The Snake House was packed, echoing with squeals. Shelby didn't seem to mind the elbow-to-elbow proposition as she maneuvered her way to a fat python.

"Looks like our representative from Nebraska."

A giggle bubbled up in Shelby's throat as she pictured the thick-necked, squinty-eyed congressman. Pleased with Alan's observation, she twisted her head to grin at him. Another inch and their lips would have made contact. She could have backed away, even though it meant stepping on a few toes. She could have simply turned her head back to the python. Instead Shelby tilted her chin so that their eyes stayed in a direct line.

What was there about him that made her want to tempt fate? she wondered. For surely that's what she would be doing if she allowed the afternoon to amount to any more than a friendly outing. He wasn't a man a woman could disentangle herself from easily, after she'd taken that last step. A man like him could quietly dominate and methodically absorb the people around him before they had any idea what was happening. For that reason alone she would have been wary of him, treating him with more caution than her other male companions. But she couldn't forget who he was—an up-and-coming young senator whose future all but demanded a bid for the top office.

No, to prevent pain on both sides, she'd keep it light. No matter how much she wanted him.

"It's crowded," she murmured as her eyes laughed into his.

"The longer we're in here…" His thighs brushed against hers as a toddler wiggled up to the glass. "The fonder I am of snakes."

"Yeah, they get to me too. It's the basic aura of evil that's so appealing." Her breasts pressed into his chest as people crowded in on all sides.

"The original sin," Alan murmured, easily catching her scent over the mingling aroma of humanity. "The serpent tempted Eve, and Eve tempted Adam."

"I've always thought Adam got off too lightly in that business," Shelby commented. Her heartbeat was fast, and not altogether steady against his, but she didn't back away. She was going to have to experience this before she understood how to prevent it. "Snakes and women took the real heat, and man came off as an innocent bystander."

"Or a creature who could rarely resist temptation in the form of a woman."

His voice had become entirely too soft. Considering it a strategic retreat, Shelby grabbed his hand and drew him away. "Let's go outside and look at the elephants."

Shelby wound her way through the people, skirting around babies in strollers as she pulled Alan outside. He would've strolled. She would always race. In the sunshine, she pushed a pair of oversize tinted glasses on her nose without slacking pace.

The aroma of animal drifted everywhere, pungent and primitive, on the breeze. You could hear them—the occasional roar, screech, or bellow. She darted along the paths, stopping at a cage, leaning against a retaining wall, taking it all in as though it were her first time. Around them were families, couples old and young, and children with dripping ice cream cones. A babble of languages flowed from both in front and behind the cages.

"There, he reminds me of you." Shelby indicated a black panther stretched in a path of sunlight, calmly watching the river of people who passed by.

"Is that so?" Alan studied the cat. "Indolent? Subdued?"

Shelby let out her smoke-edged laugh. "Oh, no, Senator. Patient, brooding. And arrogant enough to believe this confinement is nothing he can't work with." Turning, she leaned back against the barrier to consider Alan as she had considered the panther. "He's taken stock of the situation, and decided he can pretty much have his own way as things are. I wonder. . ." Her brows drew together in concentration. "I wonder just what he'd do if he were really crossed. He doesn't appear to have a temper. Cats usually don't until they're pushed too far just that one time, and then—they're deadly."

Alan gave her an odd smile before he took her hand to draw her toward the path again. "He normally sees that he's not often crossed."

Shelby tossed her head and met the smile with a bland look. "Let's go look at the monkeys. It always makes me think I'm sitting in the Senate Gallery."

"Nasty," he commented and tugged on her hair.

"I know. I couldn't help it." Briefly she rested her head on his shoulder as they walked. "I'm often not a nice person. Grant and I both seem to have inherited a streak of sarcasm—or maybe it's cynicism. Probably from my grandfather on my father's side. *He's* like one of those grizzlies we looked at. Prowling, pacing, bad-tempered."

"And you're crazy about him."

"Yeah. I'll buy you some popcorn." In a swift change of mood, she motioned toward a vendor. "You can't wander around the zoo all day without popcorn. That's second only to sitting through a double feature without some. The big one," she told the vendor as she dug a bill from the back pocket of her jeans. Shelby cradled the bucket in one arm as she stuffed the change back in her pocket. "Alan..." Changing her mind, Shelby shook her head and began to walk again.

"What?" Casually Alan reached across her for some popcorn.

"I was going to make a confession. Then I remembered I don't make them very well. We still need to see the monkeys."

"You don't really think I'm going to let a provocative statement like that slip by, do you?"

"Well...I thought the best way to discourage you was to agree to go out with you—to some place like this, which I thought would bore you to distraction—then be as obnoxious as possible."

"Have you been obnoxious?" His tone was mild and entirely too serious. "I thought you've been behaving very naturally."

"Ouch." Shelby rubbed at the figurative wound under her heart. "In any case, I get the distinct impression that I haven't discouraged you at all."

"Really?" Reaching for more popcorn, he leaned close and spoke gently in her ear. "How did you come by that?"

"Oh—" She cleared her throat. "Just a hunch."

He found that tiny show of nerves very rewarding. Yes, the puzzle was coming together, piece by careful piece. It was the way he'd always structured his life. "Odd. And not once since we've been here have I mentioned that I'd like to find a small, dim room and make love to you, over and over."

Warily Shelby slid her eyes to his. "I'd just as soon you didn't."

"All right." Alan slipped an arm around her waist. "I won't mention it while we're here."

A smile tugged at her mouth, but she shook her head. "It's not going to come to that, Alan. It can't."

"We have a fundamental disagreement." He paused on a bridge. Beneath them, swans floated haughtily. "Because to my way of thinking it has to."

"You don't understand me." Shelby turned away to watch the birds on the water because his eyes were tripping some tiny little release she hadn't even been aware was inside her. "Once I've made up my mind, I'm rock hard."

"We've more than ancestry in common." He watched the sunlight add more heat to the flames of her hair. Touching it, lightly, fingertips only, Alan wondered how it would look after they'd made love. Wild strands of fire. "I wanted you from the minute I saw you, Shelby. I want you more with every minute that passes."

She turned her head at that, surprised and unwillingly excited. It hadn't been an empty phrase or cliché. Alan MacGregor said precisely what he meant.

"And when I want something that immediately and that badly," he murmured while his fingertips strayed to her jawline, "I don't walk away from it."

Her lips parted as his thumb brushed over them. She couldn't prevent it, or the lightning-flash thrill of desire. "So—" Striving to be casual, Shelby dug out some more popcorn before she set the bucket on a bench. "You put your energies into convincing me that I want you."

He smiled. Slowly, irresistibly, he circled her neck with his fingers. "I don't have to convince you of that. What I have to convince you of," he began as he drew her closer, "is that the stand you're taking is unproductive, self-defeating, and hopeless."

She found herself weakening, wanting to be convinced. His lips hovered just above hers. Yet he was careful; even focused on her own vulnerabilities. She understood that. He'd always been circumspect in public. She'd always be careless. It annoyed her. It intrigued her too.

His eyes, so serious, so calm, seemed to cut through every logical defense she could—or would—have thrown between them. Before she could make a move toward or away, something tugged impatiently at her T-shirt.

Confused, Shelby glanced down and saw a small Oriental boy of around eight staring up at her. He began a rapid, musical spiel, complete with gestures and eye-rolling. Shelby understood the frustration if not the content.

"Slow down," she ordered, grinning as she slipped from Alan's hold to crouch in front of him. Her first thought was that he'd lost his parents. His eyes were dark and beautiful, but they were annoyed rather than frightened. Again he went off into a peal of what she suspected was Korean, then with a very adult sigh, he held up two nickels, indicating the bird feed dispenser behind him.

Ten cents, Shelby realized on a chuckle. He had the right amount but didn't understand the coinage. Before she could reach in her pocket, Alan held out a dime. Solemnly he went through a few simple gestures, showing that the two nickels put together made one dime. He saw the boy's eyes brighten with understanding before he plucked the dime out of Alan's hand and offered the two nickels. Alan's initial inclination to refuse the money altered quickly with a scan of the boy's face. Instead he accepted them, giving a slight bow. The boy gave another quick burst of Korean, returned Alan's bow, then dashed back to the dispenser.

Another man, Shelby thought as she watched the child hurl the feed to the swans, would have insisted on being magnanimous—if for no other reason than to impress the woman he was with. But Alan had understood that children have pride. He'd made the exchange of two nickels for a dime into a man-to-man business transaction instead of an adult-to-child bit of whimsy. And all without a word.

Leaning on the rail, she watched the swans race after feed, bending those slender necks, then gobbling greedily. Now and again one would honk and peck at another who edged into its territory. Alan's hands rested on the rail on either side of her. Forgetting everything but the moment, Shelby leaned back against him, letting her head find that comfortably intimate spot between his jaw and shoulder.

"It's a beautiful afternoon," she murmured.

Alan laid his hands over hers where they rested lightly. "The last time I was at the zoo, I was around twelve. My father had made one of his rare business trips to New York and insisted we go en masse." He brushed his cheek against her hair, enjoying the soft, intimate feel of it. "I felt obliged to pretend I was too old to enjoy looking at lions and tigers, yet my father had the best time of all. It's strange, that little patch of adulthood we go through when we're very young.''

''Mine lasted about six months,'' Shelby remembered. His, she knew, would never have completely dissipated. ''That's about how long I called my mother by her first name.''

''How old were you?''

''Thirteen. 'Deborah,' I would say in the cultured tones I was affecting at the time, 'I believe I'm quite old enough to have blonde streaks in my hair.' She'd say something about our discussing it very soon. Then she'd go on about how proud she was that I was mature enough to make adult decisions—how relieved she was that I wasn't spoiled or frivolous like so many girls my age.''

''And naturally you basked in that and forgot the streaks.''

''Naturally.'' With a laugh, Shelby hooked her arm through his and began to walk again. ''I don't think I appreciated just how clever she was until I was over twenty. Grant and I weren't easy children.''

''Is he like you?''

''Grant? Like me?'' Shelby pondered it a moment. ''In some ways, but he's a loner. I've never been. When Grant's with people, he observes—absorbs, really. He tucks them all away and takes them out again as he chooses. He can do without them for weeks or months at a time. I can't.''

''No, but you still take them out again as you choose. And I don't think you've ever let anyone—any man at any rate,'' he corrected, tilting his head to study her profile, ''get too close.''

Shelby flirted with an angry retort and decided on a subtler one. ''That sounds like your ego talking,'' she said mildly. ''Just because I turned you down.''

"Put me off," Alan countered as he brought her hand to his lips. "One might point out that you are here, and so am I."

"Mmm." Shelby glanced around at the flood of people as a wailing baby was carried past by a frustrated parent. "And in such intimate surroundings too."

"We're both used to crowds."

On an impulse of mischief, she stopped in the center of the path to twine her arms around his neck. "In a manner of speaking, Senator."

She expected him to laugh and pull her along again or perhaps to give an exasperated shake of his head before he disentangled himself. What she didn't expect was for him to hold her there, his lips close, hinting of promise. His eyes were level with hers, telling her very clearly where the promise would lead. There was a threat of passion, a promise of intimacy. No, she hadn't expected him to turn her own ploy against her so successfully. Perhaps for a moment Shelby had forgotten he was a man of fundamental strategies.

Against his, her heart began to thud lightly. Though the moment was brief, it touched her in every way—heart and mind and body. She couldn't hold back the regret for what she felt could never be—but she hadn't known it would be so sharp. When she drew away, it echoed in her voice and mirrored in her eyes.

"I think we'd better head back."

He ached and nearly swore from the frustration of it. "It's too damn late for that," he muttered as he steered her in the direction of the parking lot.

Shelby lifted a brow at the tone. Annoyance—it was the first time she'd heard it from him. She thought she'd caught a flicker or two in his eyes before, but it had been so quickly banked she couldn't be sure. Well then, she mused, perhaps that was the key. She would annoy him enough that he would go away.

Her skin was still warm—too warm and too tender. At the rate she was weakening, she would find herself involved with him whether she wanted it or not. Perhaps the real problem was she already was involved. The fact that they weren't lovers didn't stop him from drawing on her thoughts and her feelings. A successful break was going to hurt, but it would hurt less if it was quick and soon.

So, she would have to get under his skin. Shelby gave a smile that was more of a grimace as she stepped into his car. If there was one thing she could do well when she put her mind to it, it was to get under someone's skin.

"Well, that was fun," she said lightly as he maneuvered out of the lot. "I'm really glad you talked me into going out. My day was a blank page until seven."

That long, quiet moment lingered in his mind even as it lingered in Shelby's. Alan shifted, hoping to ease the thudding in the pit of his stomach. "Always happy to help someone fill in a few empty spaces." Alan controlled the speed of the car through force of will. Holding her hadn't soothed him but rather had only served to remind him how much time had passed since he had last held her.

"Actually you're an easy man to be with, Alan, for a politician." *Easy?* Shelby repeated to herself as she pressed the button to lower her window. Her blood was still throbbing from a meeting of eyes that had lasted less than ten seconds. If he was any *easier,* she'd be head over heels in love with him and headed for disaster. "I mean, you're not really pompous."

He shot her a look, long and cool, that boosted her confidence. "No?" he murmured after a humming silence.

"Hardly at all." Shelby sent him a smile. "Why, I'd probably vote for you myself."

Alan paused at a red light, studying it thoughtfully before he turned to her. "Your insults aren't as subtle today, Shelby."

"Insults?" She gave him a bland stare. "Odd, I thought it was more flattery. Isn't a vote what it all comes down to? Votes, and that all-encompassing need to win."

The light stayed green for five full seconds before he cruised through it. "Be careful."

A nerve, she thought, hating herself more than a little. "You're a little touchy. That's all right." She brushed at the thigh of her jeans. "I don't mind a little oversensitivity."

"The subject of my sensitivity isn't the issue, but you're succeeding in being obnoxious."

"My, my, aren't we all Capitol Hill all of a sudden." Deliberately she looked at her watch as he pulled into the alleyway next to her building. "That was good timing. I'll have a chance to take a bath and a change before I go out." Shelby leaned over to give him a careless kiss on the cheek before she slipped from the car. "Thanks, Alan. *Ciao.*"

Despising herself, Shelby made it all the way to the top landing before he caught her arm. She fixed a mildly surprised expression on her face before she turned her head.

"What the hell is this all about?" he demanded. There was enough pressure on her arm to make her turn fully around.

"What the hell is all what about?"

"Don't play games, Shelby."

She sighed sharply, as if bored. "It was a nice afternoon, a . . . change of pace for both of us, I imagine." She unlocked her apartment door.

Alan tightened his grip fractionally to prevent her from slipping inside. Temper—he never, or rarely, gave in to it. It was a by-product of his heritage, the stock-in-trade of his family, but he'd always been the controlled one. The clearheaded one. He fought to remember it. "And?"

"And?" Shelby repeated, lifting both brows. "There is no *and,* Alan. We spent a couple of hours at the zoo, had a few laughs. That certainly doesn't mean I'm required to sleep with you."

She saw the anger, volatile and fierce, sweep into his eyes. A bit stunned at the strength of it, Shelby took an automatic step back. Her throat went dry instantly. Had that been sleeping in there the whole time? she wondered.

"Do you think that's all I want?" he asked in a deadly voice as he backed her into the door. "If I only wanted you in bed, you'd have been there." His hand came up to circle her throat as she stared at the livid fury on his face.

"There's the matter of what I want," she managed, surprised that her voice was thready and breathless. Was it fear? she asked herself swiftly. Or was it excitement?

"The hell with what you want."

When he took a step closer, Shelby pressed back so the door gave way. She would have stumbled if he hadn't been quick enough to grab her. Then they were just inside, with her body crushed close against his, her hands on his shoulders, for once indecisive.

She tossed back her head, furious that her knees had liquefied with fear while her blood pumped hard and fast with pure desire. "Alan, you can't—"

"Can't?" His hand was in her hair, dragging her head back further. It poured into him fluidly—anger, resentment, passion. He'd never felt all at once. "I can. We both know I can now, and could have before." And I should have, he told himself as fury and frustration took over. "You want me right now; I can see it."

She shook her head but couldn't dislodge his hand. How could she have forgotten the panther so soon? "No, I don't."

"Do you think you can take shots at what I do, at what I am, with impunity, Shelby?" The arm around her waist tightened so that she struggled not to gasp. "Do you think you can push me so far and not pay any price?"

She swallowed, but her throat stayed dry. "You're acting as though I've encouraged you when I've done precisely the opposite," she told him in what almost succeeded in being a mildly annoyed tone. "Let me go, Alan."

"When I'm ready."

His mouth came down toward hers. Shelby sucked in her breath—whether in protest or anticipation, she wasn't sure. But he stopped, just short of contact so she was trembling. All she could see in his eyes was fury, and her own reflection. Yes, she'd forgotten the panther, and that wicked, seething temper of the Brontë heroes he'd first reminded her of.

"Do you think you're what I want? What I can rationally, easily, say I want? You're everything but what suits me. You flout everything that's vital to my life."

That hurt. Though it was precisely what she'd set out to do, it hurt that he could say it. "I'm exactly what I am," she tossed back. "Exactly what I want to be. Why don't you leave me alone and go find one of those cool blondes who look so perfect in an Oscar de la Renta? They're tailor-made for a senator's companion. I don't want any part of it."

"Maybe not." The anger was building. He'd never felt anything build so quickly. "Maybe not. But tell me—" His grip tightened. "Tell me you don't want me."

Her breath came quickly; short pants that couldn't seem to fill her lungs. She wasn't even aware that her fingers had dug into his shoulders or that her tongue, in a swift, nervous movement, darted out to moisten her lips. Shelby had always known there was a time and a place for lies.

"I don't want you."

But the denial ended on a moan of shivering excitement as his mouth captured hers. This wasn't the patient, endless seduction of a kiss he'd first treated her to, but its antithesis. Hard, ruthless, his lips dominated hers as no one's had ever done. As no man had ever dared. Then she was spinning, and groping for the guideposts that were no longer there.

She could taste his anger and met it with a helpless passion that built too quickly to be controlled. She could feel his fury and met it with a fire that flamed too high to be banked. There was no sharp stab of regret. She was where she wanted to be. The fingers that gripped his shoulders urged him to demand more, and as he demanded, she took.

Alan twisted her closer, forgetting the gentleness that had always been an innate part of his lovemaking. Her mouth was wild under his, greedy for possession. But this time he wasn't content with it. His hand snaked under her shirt to find her.

So slim, so soft, yet her heart pounded under his roaming palm with the strength of a marathon runner's. She strained against him, moaning what might have been his name. Her taste was as wild and free as her scent, inciting the urgency to drum in him until it was a pounding. He could take her—on the floor or where they stood—in seconds or in an hour. Just knowing it sent an agony of desire rocketing through him. This was no yielding, but rather passion to passion, fire to fire. He'd never subdue her, but he could have her.

And if he took her now, though she was willing, he risked having nothing when it was done. He risked making that careless, cutting remark of hers no less than the truth.

On an oath uncharacteristically savage, Alan yanked her away. His eyes, when they met hers, were no less angry than they had been, and no less hard. The look held in silence but for the sound of unsteady breathing. Without a word, he turned and strode through the open door.

Chapter Five

She tried not to think about it. Shelby flipped through the magazine section of the Sunday paper with her feet propped up and her second cup of coffee still steaming and really tried not to think about it. Moshe sprawled across the back of the sofa as if he were reading over her shoulder, his nose occasionally twitching from the scent of her coffee. Shelby sipped and skimmed an article on French cooking on a budget.

She couldn't help but think about it.

It had been entirely her fault; she couldn't deny it. Being rude and nasty wasn't something she set out to do often, but she'd done a good job of it. Hurting someone else was something she usually did only in the blind heat of rage. But she couldn't deny there'd been hurt as well as anger in Alan's eyes. Even though her purpose had been self-preservation, Shelby was having a difficult time forgiving herself.

Do you think you're what I want?

No. Shelby sat back, cupping her mug in both hands. No, she'd known right from the start that she hadn't suited him, his image, any more than he'd suited hers. Yet she'd sensed something about him, and herself, that first evening on the Writes' terrace. They'd seen too much in each other too quickly. Something had been nudging at the back of her mind even then. *He could be the one.* Silly fancies for a woman who'd never considered she'd wanted anyone to be *the one,* but she hadn't been able to shake it off.

She wondered if she'd shaken Alan off. Certainly she'd deserved his fury and the icy temper in his eyes when he'd walked back through her doorway. She had the power to bring that out in him. It was frightening and somehow...yes, somehow seducing. But she could turn vicious with it; that was something else. The viciousness came again from self-preservation when she sensed his power over her was too strong. So, perhaps she'd also deserved, though it was no easier to live with today, the aching and the wanting he'd left her with.

She circled her tongue over her lips, remembering. There were two sides of Alan MacGregor, she mused. The even-tempered and reasonable, and the hard and the ruthless. It only made him more appealing. More dangerous, she added grimly.

Setting aside the mug, Shelby snapped the paper into place and tried to concentrate. After all, she'd pushed him away, just as she'd set out to do. There was no use feeling miserable about it. In almost the same breath, she tossed the paper aside and leapt up to pace. She wasn't going to call and apologize. It would only complicate things.

Still, if she made it clear it was a formal apology and nothing more... No, that wasn't smart, she reminded herself with a shake of the head. Worse, it was weak and wishy-washy. She'd made her decision. Shelby had always prided herself on knowing her own mind and sticking to it.

Her gaze alighted on the balloons jumbled on her kitchen table. They'd lost the power to hang high in the air, and lay comfortably now, like a reminder of a happy celebration. Her breath came out in a sigh. She should have popped them and tossed out the corpses. Shelby ran a finger down a squishy yellow sphere. It was too late now.

If she called and absolutely refused to get involved in a conversation—just an apology and nothing more. Three minutes. Shelby gnawed on her lip and wondered if she could find her egg timer. Her conscience would be clear in a few polite sentences. What could happen in three minutes over the phone? She glanced down at the balloons again. A lot, she remembered. It had been a phone call that had started the whole mess the day before.

Even as she stood, irresolute, someone knocked at the door. She glanced over quickly, anticipation shimmering. Before the knock could sound twice, she was jerking the door open.

"I was just— Oh, hello, Mama."

"I'm sorry I'm not who you were hoping for." Deborah gave Shelby a quick peck on the cheek before she strolled inside.

"It's better that you weren't," Shelby murmured as she closed the door. "Well, I'll get you some coffee," she said with a flash of a smile. "It's not often you drop in on a Sunday morning."

"You can make it a half a cup if you're expecting someone."

"I'm not." Shelby's tone was flat and final.

Deborah pondered her daughter's back a moment, speculating. With a rueful shake of her head, she wondered why she bothered. She hadn't been able to outguess Shelby in over ten years. "If you're not doing anything this afternoon, perhaps you'd like to go with me to see that new exhibit of Flemish art at the National Gallery.

Shelby swore ripely, then stuck her thumb knuckle into her mouth.

"Oh, did you burn yourself. Let me—"

"It's nothing," Shelby said too sharply and swore again. "I'm sorry," she managed in a calmer voice. "I just spilled a little on me, that's all. Sit down, Mama." In an almost violent gesture, she swept the balloons off the table and onto the floor.

"Well, that hasn't changed," Deborah observed mildly. "You still have your own way of tidying up." She waited until Shelby sat across from her. "Is something wrong?"

"Wrong?" Shelby nursed her thumb a moment longer. "No, why?"

"You're rarely jumpy." Stirring her coffee, Deborah leveled one of her long, steady stares. "Have you seen the paper this morning?"

"Of course." Shelby folded her legs under her. "I wouldn't miss Grant's Sunday edition."

"No, I didn't mean that."

Vaguely interested, Shelby lifted her brows. "I glanced at the front page and didn't see anything I wanted to dip into too deeply first thing in the morning. Did I miss something?"

"Apparently." Without another word, Deborah rose and went over to the sofa. She ruffled through the disorder of Shelby's paper until she found the section she wanted. There was a half-smile on her lips as she walked over to drop the paper, faceup, in front of her daughter. Shelby looked down and said nothing.

There was a well-framed, very clear picture of her and Alan as they stood on the bridge overlooking the swans. Shelby remembered the moment: she had leaned back against him, resting her head between his shoulder and jaw. The photograph had captured that instant and a look of quiet contentment on her face that she wasn't certain had ever been there before.

The column beneath it was brief, giving her name and age, a mention of her father, and a quick plug for her shop. It also touched on Alan's campaign on housing for the homeless before it drifted into speculation on their relationship. There was nothing offensive in the short, chatty little slice of Washington gossip. She was surprised by a sharp stab of resentment as she scanned the story.

She'd been right, Shelby told herself as her gaze skimmed back to the picture. The eighth of a page proved that she'd been right from the beginning. Politics, in all its aspects, would always be between them. They'd had their afternoon as ordinary people, but it hadn't lasted. It never would.

Deliberately Shelby pushed the paper aside before she picked up her coffee. "Well, I wouldn't be surprised if I had quite a crowd on Monday morning thanks to this. I had a woman drive down from Baltimore last winter after she'd seen a picture of me with Myra's nephew." She made herself sip, aware that she was dangerously close to rambling. "It's a good thing I went on a binge last week and stocked the back room. Do you want a doughnut to go with that coffee? I think I might have one somewhere."

"Shelby." Deborah laid both her hands on her daughter's before Shelby could rise. The half-smile had been replaced by a look of concern. "I've never known you to mind this kind of publicity. That's Grant's phobia, not yours."

"Why should I mind?" Shelby countered, struggling to keep her fingers from curling into fists. "If anything, it should bring me a few sales. Some enterprising tourist recognized Alan and cashed in, that's all. It's harmless."

"Yes." With a slow nod, Deborah soothed the agitated hands beneath hers. "It is."

"No, it's not!" Shelby retorted with sudden passion. "It's not harmless, none of it." She sprang up from the table to whirl around the room as Deborah had seen her do countless times before. "I can't cope with it. I *won't* cope with it." She kicked at a sneaker that got in her way. "Why the hell couldn't he be a nuclear physicist or own bowling alleys? Why does he have to look at me as if he's known me all my life and doesn't mind all the flaws? I don't want him to pull at me this way. I won't have it!" On a final burst of rage, she swooped the scattered sections of the paper from the sofa to the floor.

"It doesn't matter." Shelby stopped, dragging a hand through her hair as she leveled her breathing. "It doesn't matter," she repeated. "I've made up my mind in any case, so..." Shaking her head, she walked back to the stove to fetch the coffeepot. "Shall I heat that up for you?"

Too used to Shelby to be confused by the outburst, Deborah nodded. "Just a touch. What have you made up your mind about, Shelby?"

"That I'm not going to get involved with him." After replacing the pot, Shelby came back to sit down. "Why don't we have lunch in the Gallery cafeteria?"

"All right." Deborah sipped her coffee. "Did you have a good time at the zoo?"

Shelby shrugged and stared into her mug. "It was a nice day." She brought the mug to her lips, then set it aside without drinking.

Deborah glanced down at the picture again. When was the last time she'd seen Shelby look serene? Had she ever? Oh, perhaps, she mused with a quick, almost forgotten pang, when a little girl had sat with her father sharing some private thought. Deborah held back a sigh and feigned an interest in her coffee.

"I suppose you've made your position clear to Senator MacGregor."

"I told Alan right from the start that I wouldn't even date him."

"You came with him to the Ditmeyers' last week."

"That was different." She toyed restlessly with the edges of the paper. "And yesterday was just a lapse."

"He's not your father, Shelby."

Gray eyes lifted, so unexpectedly tormented that Deborah reached for her hand again. "He's so much like him," Shelby whispered. "It's frightening. The tranquillity, the dedication, that spark that tells you he's going to reach for the top and probably get it, unless..." She broke off and shut her eyes. Unless some maniac with an obscure cause and a gun stopped him. "Oh, God, I think I'm falling in love with him, and I want to run."

Deborah tightened her grip. "Where?"

"Anywhere." Taking a long, steadying breath, Shelby opened her eyes. "I don't want to fall in love with him for dozens of reasons. We're nothing alike, he and I."

For the first time since she had handed Shelby the paper, Deborah smiled. "Should you be?"

"Don't confuse me when I'm trying to be logical." Settling a bit, Shelby smiled back. "Mama, I'd drive the man crazy in a week. I could never ask him to acclimate to my sort of life. I'd never be able to acclimate to his. You only need to talk with him for a few minutes to see that he has an ordered mind, the kind that works like a superior chess game. He'd be accustomed to having his meals at certain times, knowing precisely what shirts he'd sent to be laundered."

"Darling, even you must realize how foolish that sounds."

"By itself, maybe it would." Her gaze drifted to the balloons that lay on the floor. "But when you add in everything else."

"By everything else, you meant the fact that he's a politician. Shelby..." Deborah waited until her daughter's eyes met hers. "You can't special-order the kind of man you fall in love with."

"I'm not going to fall in love with him." Her face settled into stubborn lines. "I like my life just as it is. No one's going to make me change it before I'm ready. Come on." She was up and moving again. "We'll go look at your Flemish art, then I'll treat you to lunch."

Deborah watched as Shelby dashed around the apartment looking for shoes. No, she didn't wish her daughter pain, Deborah thought again, but she knew it was coming. Shelby would have to deal with it.

Alan sat behind the huge antique desk in his study with the window open at his back. He could just smell the lilacs blooming on the bush in the little patch of yard outside. He remembered there had been the scent of lilacs the first evening he'd met Shelby. But he wouldn't think of her now.

Spread out on his desk were responses and information on the volunteer shelters he was campaigning for. He had a meeting with the mayor of Washington the following day and could only hope it went as well as his discussion with the mayor of Boston had. He had the facts—his staff had been working on compiling the information he needed for weeks. He had the pictures in front of him. Alan lifted one of two men sharing the tatters of a blanket in a doorway near 14th and Belmont. It wasn't just sad, it was inexcusable. Shelter was the first basic need.

It was one thing to concentrate on the causes—unemployment, recession, the bugs in the welfare system—and another to watch people live without the most elemental needs met while the wheels of social reform slowly turned. His idea was to provide the needs—shelter, food, clothing—in return for labor and time. No free rides, no sting of charity.

But he needed funds—and just as important—he needed volunteers. He'd put things in motion in Boston after a long, at times frustrating, battle, but it was too soon to show substantial results. He was going to have to depend on the information compiled by his staff and his own powers of persuasion. If he could add the mayor's influence, Alan thought he might just be able to wrangle the federal funds he wanted. Eventually.

Stacking the papers, Alan slipped them inside his briefcase. There was nothing more he could do until the following day. And he was expecting a visitor—he checked his watch—in ten minutes. Alan leaned back in the comfortably worn leather chair and allowed his mind to empty.

He'd always been able to relax in this room. The paneling was dark and gleaming, the ceiling high. In the winter, he kept a low fire going in the rosy marble fireplace. Lining the mantel were pictures in the odd-shaped antique frames he collected. His family—from tintypes of his great-grandparents who'd never stepped off Scottish soil, to snapshots of his brother and sister. He'd be adding one of his niece or nephew when his sister, Rena, had the baby.

Alan glanced up at the picture of an elegant fair-haired woman with laughing eyes and a stubborn mouth. Strange how many shades hair came in, he mused. Rena's hair was nothing like Shelby's. Shelby's was all undisciplined curls of fire and flame.

Undisciplined. The word suited her—and attracted him despite his better judgment. Handling her would be a lifelong challenge. Having her would be a constant surprise. Strange that a man who'd always preferred the well-ordered and logical would now know his life wouldn't be complete without disruption.

He glanced around the room—walls of books, meticulously filed and stacked, a pale-gray carpet that showed signs of wear but no dirt, the prim Victorian sofa in deep burgundy. The room was organized and neat—like his life. He was asking for a whirlwind. Alan had no interest in subduing it, just in experiencing it.

When the doorbell rang, he glanced at his watch again. Myra was right on time.

"Good morning, McGee." Myra breezed in with a smile for Alan's sturdy Scottish butler.

"Good morning, Mrs. Ditmeyer." McGee was six-two, solid as a brick wall, and closing in on seventy. He'd been Alan's family butler for thirty years before leaving Hyannis Port for Georgetown at his own insistence. Mister Alan would need him, he'd said in his gravel-edged burr. That, as far as McGee was concerned, had been that.

"I don't suppose you made any of those marvelous scones?"

"With clotted cream," McGee told her, coming as close as he ever did to cracking a smile.

"Ah, McGee, I adore you. Alan . . ." Myra held out her hand as he came down the hall. "So sweet of you to let me bother you on a Sunday."

"It's never a bother, Myra." He kissed her cheek before leading her into the parlor.

This room was done in quiet, masculine colors—ecrus and creams with an occasional touch of deep green. The furniture was mostly Chippendale, the carpet a faded Oriental. It was a calm, comfortable room with the surprise of a large oil painting depicting a storm-tossed landscape—all jagged mountains, boiling clouds, and threatening lightning—on the south wall. Myra had always considered it an interesting, and telling, addition.

With a sigh, she sat in a high-back chair and slipped out of her shoes—skinny heels in the same shocking pink as her bag. "What a relief," she murmured. "I simply can't convince myself to buy the right size. What a price we pay for vanity." Her toes wriggled comfortably. "I got the sweetest note from Rena," she continued, rubbing one foot over the other to restore circulation as she smiled at Alan. "She wanted to know when Herbert and I are coming up to Atlantic City to lose money in her casino."

"I dropped a bit myself the last time I was up there." Alan sat back knowing Myra would get to the point of her visit in her own time.

"How's Caine? What a naughty boy he always was," she went on before Alan could answer. "Whoever thought he'd turn out to be a brilliant attorney?"

"Life's full of surprises," Alan murmured. Caine had been the naughty boy and he the disciplined one. Why should he think of that now?

"Oh, how true. Ah, here goes my diet. Thank God," she announced as McGee entered with a tray. "I'll pour, McGee, bless you." Myra lifted the Meissen teapot, busying herself while Alan watched her with amusement. Whatever she was up to, she was going to enjoy her scones and tea first. "How I envy you your butler," she told Alan as she handed him a cup. "Did you know I tried to steal him away from your parents twenty years ago?"

"No, I didn't." Alan grinned. "But then McGee's much too discreet to have mentioned it."

"And too loyal to succumb to my clever bribes. It was the first time I tasted one of these." Myra bit into a scone and rolled her eyes. "Naturally I thought it was the cook's doing and considered snatching her, but when I found out the scones were McGee's...ah, well, my consolation is that if I'd succeeded, I'd be as big as an elephant. Which reminds me." She dusted her fingers on a napkin. "I noticed you've taken an interest in elephants."

Alan lifted a brow as he sipped. So this was it. "I'm always interested in the opposing party," he said mildly.

"I'm not talking about political symbols," Myra retorted archly. "Did you have a good time at the zoo?"

"You've seen the paper."

"Of course. I must say the two of you looked very good together. I thought you would." She took a self-satisfied sip of tea. "Was Shelby annoyed by the picture?"

"I don't know." Alan's brows lowered in puzzlement. He'd lived his life in the public eye too long to give it any more than a passing thought. "Should she be?"

"Normally no; but then, Shelby's prone to feel and do the unexpected. I'm not prying, Alan—yes, I am," she corrected with an irresistible grin. "But only because I've known you both since you were children. I'm very fond of both you and Shelby." Giving in to temptation with only a token struggle, she helped herself to another scone. "I was quite pleased when I saw the picture this morning."

Enjoying her healthy appetite as well as her irrepressible meddling, Alan smiled back at her. "Why?"

"Actually..." Myra helped herself to a generous spoonful of cream. "I shouldn't be. I was planning to get you two together myself. It's really put my nose out of joint that you handled matters without me, even though I approve of the end result."

Knowing the way her mind worked, Alan leaned back against the sofa, resting one arm over the back. "An afternoon at the zoo doesn't equal matrimony."

"Spoken like a true politician." With a sigh of pure gastronomic pleasure, Myra sat back. "If I could only wrangle the recipe for these scones out of McGee..."

Alan gave her a smile that was more amused than apologetic. "I don't think so."

"Ah, well. I happened to be in Shelby's shop when a basket of strawberries was delivered," she added casually. "You wouldn't happen to know anything about that, would you, dear?"

"Strawberries?" Alan gave another noncommittal smile. "I'm quite fond of them myself."

"I'm much too clever to be conned," Myra told him, shaking her finger. "And I know you entirely too well. A man like you doesn't send baskets of strawberries or spend afternoons at the zoo unless he's infatuated."

"I'm not infatuated with Shelby," Alan corrected mildly as he sipped his tea. "I'm in love with her."

Myra's planned retort came out as a huff of breath. "Well then," she managed. "That was quicker than even I expected."

"It was instant," Alan murmured, not quite as easy now that he'd made the statement.

"Lovely." Myra leaned forward to pat his knee. "I can't think of anyone who deserves the shock of love at first sight more."

He had to laugh, though his mood was no longer light. "Shelby's not having it."

"What do you mean she's not?" Myra demanded with a frown.

"Just that." It still hurt, Alan discovered as he set down his tea. The memory of her words, that careless tone, still slashed him. "She isn't even interested in seeing me."

"Poppycock." Myra sniffed and set aside a half-eaten scone. "I was with her when she got those strawberries. And I know Shelby nearly as well as I know you." She punctuated the statement with a quick jab at his knee. "It was the first time in my life I'd seen her look quite that way.''

Alan stared into middle distance a moment, considering. ''She's a very stubborn woman,'' he said thoughtfully. ''She's determined to avoid any sort of personal entanglement with me because of my profession.''

''Ah, I see.'' Myra nodded slowly as she began to tap a long red nail against the arm of the chair. ''I should have known.''

''She's not indifferent,'' Alan murmured, thinking aloud as he remembered the way her mouth had heated beneath his. ''Just obstinate.''

''Not obstinate,'' Myra corrected, bringing him back. ''Frightened. She was very close to her father.''

''I gathered that, Myra, and I understand it must have been hard, very hard, to lose him the way she did, but I can't see what it has to do with us.'' His impatience was edging through, and his frustration. Alan rose, no longer able to sit still, and paced the room. ''If her father had been an architect, would it make sense for her to write architects off?'' He dragged a hand through his hair in a rare gesture of exasperation. ''Dammit, Myra, it's bloody ridiculous for her to shut me out because her father was a senator.''

''You're being logical, Alan,'' Myra said patiently. ''Shelby rarely is—unless you consider that she uses her own brand of logic. She adored Robert Campbell, and I don't use the word lightly.'' She paused again, her sympathies aroused for both of them. ''She was only eleven years old when he was shot and killed not twenty feet away from her.''

Alan stopped pacing to slowly turn around. ''She was there?''

"Both her and Grant." Myra set aside her cup, wishing her memory weren't quite so clear. "It was a miracle that Deborah managed to keep the press from exploiting that angle. She used every contact she had."

He felt a flash of empathy, so stunning and sharp it left him dazed. "Oh, God, I can't even imagine how horrible it must have been for her."

"She didn't speak—not a word—for days. I spent a lot of time with her as Deborah was trying to cope with her own grief, the children's, the press." She shook her head, remembering Deborah's quietly desperate attempts to reach her daughter, and Shelby's mute withdrawal. "It was a dreadful time, Alan. Political assassinations add public scope to our private grief."

A long, weary sigh escaped—a sound she rarely gave in to. "Shelby didn't break down until the day after the funeral. She mourned like—like an animal," Myra said. "Raw, wild grief that lasted as long as her silence had. Then she snapped out of it, maybe too well."

He wasn't certain he wanted to hear more, picturing the child that was the woman he loved shattered, lost, and groping. He'd have been in his second year at Harvard then, secure in his world, within easy reach of his family. Even at thirty-five, he'd never suffered any devastating loss. His father—Alan tried to imagine the sudden violent loss of the robust and vital Daniel MacGregor. It was too searing a pain to be felt. He stared out the window at spring-green leaves and fresh blossoms.

"What did she do?"

"She lived—using every drop of that surplus of energy she's always had. Once when she was sixteen," Myra remembered, "Shelby told me that life was a game called Who Knows? and that she was going to give everything a try before it played a trick on her."

"That sounds like her," Alan murmured.

"Yes, and all in all she's the most well-adjusted creature I know. Content with her own flaws—perhaps proud of a few of them. But Shelby's a vortex of emotion. The more she uses, the more she has. Perhaps she's never really stopped grieving."

"She can't dictate her emotions," Alan said with fresh frustration as Myra's words ate at him. "No matter how much her father's death affected her."

"No, but Shelby would think she could."

"She thinks too damn much," he muttered.

"No, she *feels* too damn much. She won't be an easy woman to love, or to live with."

Alan forced himself to sit again. "I stopped wanting an easy woman when I met Shelby." Things were a bit clearer now and therefore more easily solved. Specific, tangible problems were his specialty. He began to play back Shelby's words to him of the afternoon before—the biting carelessness. He remembered, as he forced himself to be calm, that quick flicker of regret he'd seen in her eyes. "She gave me my walking papers yesterday," he said softly.

Myra set down her tea with a snap. "What nonsense. The girl needs—" She interrupted herself with another huff. "If you're that easily discouraged, I don't know why I bother. Young people expect everything to be handed to them on a platter, I suppose. The first stumbling block, and it's all over. Your father," she continued, heating up, "could find a way to bulldoze through anything. And your mother, whom I've always thought you took after, simply eased her way through any problem without creating a ripple. A fine president you'll make," she finished grumpily. "I'm going to reconsider voting for you."

"I'm not running for president," Alan said as soberly as his grin would allow.

"Yet."

"Yet," he agreed. "And I'm going to marry Shelby."

"Oh." Deflated, Myra sat back again. "Perhaps I'll vote for you after all. When?"

Staring at the ceiling, Alan considered, calculating, turning over angles. "I've always liked Hyannis Port in the fall," he mused. Shifting his gaze, he gave Myra his slow, serious smile. "Shelby should enjoy getting married in a drafty castle, don't you think?"

Chapter Six

A week was only seven days. Shelby made it through almost six of them by pretending she wasn't going crazy. By midafternoon on Friday, she was running low on excuses for her bad temper and absentmindedness.

She wasn't sleeping well; that's why she was listless. She wasn't sleeping well because she'd been so busy—at the shop and with a round of social engagements. Shelby hadn't turned down any invitation that had come her way all week. Because she was listless, or overtired or whatever, she was forgetting things—like eating. Because she had thrown her system off schedule, she was cranky. And because she was cranky, she didn't have any appetite.

Shelby had managed this circular sort of justification for days without once bringing the reason back to Alan. Several times she told herself she hadn't thought of him at all. Not once. As it happened, Shelby began to tell herself several times a day that she hadn't thought of him. Once she was so pleased with herself for not giving him a thought, she smashed a delft-blue flowerpot against her workroom wall.

This was so blatantly out of character that Shelby was forced to resort to her circular route of rationale all over again.

She worked when she could—late at night when she couldn't bear to lie awake in bed, early in the morning for the same reason. When she went out, she was almost desperately bright and cheerful so that a few of her closer friends began to watch her with some concern. Filling her time became of paramount importance. Then she would forget that she'd made arrangements to meet friends for dinner and bury herself in her workroom.

It could be the weather, Shelby mused as she sat behind the counter with her chin on her hand. The radio gave her music and welcome noise, with regular announcements that the rain would end by Sunday. To Shelby, Sunday was light-years away.

Rain depressed a lot of people, and just because it had never depressed her before didn't mean it wasn't doing so this time. Two solid days of streaming, soaking rain could make anyone grumpy. Brooding, Shelby watched through the shop window as it continued to fall.

Rain wasn't good for business, she decided. She'd had a little more than a trickle of customers that day and the day before. Normally she would have closed up shop with a philosophical shrug and found something else to do. But she stayed, frowning, as gloomy as the rain.

Maybe she'd just go away for the weekend, she thought. Hop on a plane and shoot up to Maine and surprise Grant. Oh, he'd be furious, Shelby thought with the first real smile she'd managed in days. He'd give her hell for dropping in unannounced. Then they'd have such a good time badgering each other. No one made bickering as much fun as Grant.

Grant saw too much, Shelby remembered with a sigh. He'd know something was wrong, and though he was fierce about his own privacy, he'd pick at her until she told him everything. She could tell her mother—at least part of it—but she couldn't tell Grant. Maybe because he understood too well.

So... Shelby gave another long sigh and considered her options. She could stay in Georgetown and be miserable over the weekend or she could leave. It might be fun to just toss a few things in the car and drive until she left the rain behind. Skyline Drive in Virginia or the beach at Nags Head. A change of scene, she decided abruptly. Any scene at all.

Impulsively Shelby jumped up and prepared to turn over the *Closed* sign. The door opened, letting in a *whoosh* of chilled air and a scattering of rain. A woman in a yellow slicker and boots closed the door with a slam.

"Miserable weather," she said cheerfully.

"The worst," Shelby pushed the impatience back. Ten minutes before she'd considered standing on one foot and juggling to attract a customer. "Is there something in particular I can show you?"

"I'll just poke around."

Oh, sure, Shelby thought, pinning on an amiable smile. I could be halfway to sunshine by the time she finishes poking. Shelby considered telling the woman she had ten minutes. "Take your time," she said instead.

"I found out about your shop from a neighbor." The woman stopped to study a fat speckled pot suitable for a patio or terrace. "She'd bought a coffee set I admired. A very pale blue with pansies dashed over it."

"Yes, I remember it." Shelby managed to keep the friendly smile in place as she watched the woman's back. "I don't do duplicates, but if you're interested in coffee sets, I have one along similar lines." Scanning the shop, she tried to remember where she'd set it.

"Actually it wasn't the specific set as much as the workmanship that caught my eye. She told me you make all your stock yourself."

"That's right." Shelby forced herself not to fidget and concentrated on the woman. Attractive, mid-thirties, friendly. The sleek brunette hair had a subtle and sophisticated frosting of wheat-toned blond. Shelby wished the woman would go back to wherever she came from, then was immediately furious with herself. "I have my wheel in the back room," she went on, making more of an effort. "I do all the firing and glazing there as well."

The customer crouched down beside a standing urn, studying it meticulously. "Do you ever use molds?"

"Once in a while, for something like that bull there, or the gnome, but I prefer the wheel."

"You know, you have a marvelous talent—and quite a supply of energy." Rising, the woman ran a fingertip down the spout of a coffeepot. "I can imagine how much time and patience it takes to produce all this, over and above the skill."

"Thank you. I suppose when you enjoy something, you don't think about the time it takes."

"*Mmm,* I know. I'm a decorator." Walking over, she handed Shelby a business card. *Maureen Francis, Interior Design.* "I'm doing my own apartment at the moment, and I have to have that pot, that urn, and that vase." She pointed to each of her choices before turning back to Shelby. "Can I give you a deposit and have you hold them for me until Monday? I don't want to cart them around in the rain."

"Of course. I'll have them packed up for you when you're ready for them."

"Terrific." Maureen pulled a checkbook out of the leather hobo bag she carried. "You know, I have a feeling we're going to be doing quite a bit of business. I've only been in D.C. about a month, but I do have a couple of interesting jobs coming up." She glanced up with another smile before she continued to write out the check. "I like to use handcrafted pieces in my work. There's nothing worse than a room that shrieks of professional decorator."

The statement, from someone who made her living at it, intrigued Shelby. She forgot her inclination to rush Maureen out the door. "Where are you from?"

"Chicago. I worked for a large firm there—ten years." She ripped off the check and handed it to Shelby. "I got the itch to strike out on my own."

Nodding, Shelby finished making out her receipt. "Are you any good?"

Maureen blinked at the blunt question, then grinned. "I'm very good."

Shelby studied her face a moment—candid eyes, a touch of humor. Going, as always, on impulse, she scrawled a name and address on the back of the receipt. "Myra Ditmeyer," Shelby told her. "If anyone who's anyone in the area is toying with redecorating, she'll know. Tell her I gave you her name."

A bit stunned, Maureen stared down at the receipt. She'd been in D.C. long enough to know of Myra Ditmeyer. "Thanks."

"Myra'll expect your life history in lieu of a percentage, but—" Shelby broke off as the door to the shop opened again. She had the unexpected, and for her, unique experience of going completely blank.

Alan closed the door, then calmly stripped out of his wet coat before he crossed to her. Giving Maureen a friendly nod, he cupped Shelby's chin, leaned over the counter, and kissed her. "I brought you a present."

"No!" The quick panic in her voice infuriated her. After shoving at his hand, she stepped back. "Go away."

Alan leaned on the counter as he turned to Maureen. "Is that any way to act when someone brings you a present?"

"Well, I . . ." Maureen looked from Shelby to Alan before she gave a noncommital shrug.

"Of course it isn't," he went on as if she'd agreed. He drew a box out of his coat pocket and set it on the counter.

"I'm not going to open it." Shelby looked down at the box only because it prevented her from looking at Alan. She wouldn't risk having her mind swept clean again so soon. "And I'm closed."

"Not for fifteen minutes. Shelby's often rude," he told Maureen. "Would you like to see what I brought her?"

Torn between a desire to run for cover and creeping curiosity, Maureen hesitated a moment too long. Alan plucked off the cover of the box and pulled out a small piece of colored glass in the shape of a rainbow. Shelby's hand was halfway to it before she stopped herself.

"Dammit, Alan," How could he have known how badly she'd needed to see a rainbow?

"That's her traditional response," he told Maureen. "It means she likes it."

"I told you to stop sending me things."

"I didn't send it," he pointed out as he dropped the rainbow in her hand. "I brought it."

"I don't want it," she said heatedly, but her fingers curled around it. "If you weren't a thick-skinned, bone-headed MacGregor, you'd leave me alone."

"Fortunately for both of us, we share some of the same traits." He had her hand in his before she could prevent it. "Your pulse is racing again, Shelby."

Maureen cleared her throat. "Well, I think I'll just be running along." She stuffed the receipt in her bag as Shelby stared helplessly at Alan. "I'll be back Monday," she added, though neither of them acknowledged her departure. "If someone gave me a rainbow on a day like today," she commented as she headed for the door. "I'd be sunk."

Sunk, Shelby repeated silently. It wasn't until the door closed that she snapped back. "Stop it," she ordered and snatched her hand away. When she flicked off the radio, the room fell into silence, accentuated by the drumming rain. Too late, she realized she'd made her first mistake. Now it was all too apparent that her breathing wasn't as steady as it should be. "Alan, I'm closing shop."

"Good idea." He strode over to the door, flipped around the sign, then shot the bolt.

"Now, just a minute," she began furiously. "You can't—" She broke off as he began to come toward her. The calmly determined look in his eyes had her taking a step back and swallowing. "This is my shop, and you—" Her back hit the wall as he skirted around the counter.

"And *we,*" he began when he stopped directly in front of her, "are going out to dinner."

"I'm not going anywhere."

"You are," he corrected.

Shelby stared up at him, confused and pulsing. His voice hadn't been fierce or impatient. There wasn't any anger in his eyes. She'd have preferred anger to that simple, unarguable confidence. Temper made it so easy to defend with temper. If he was going to be calm, she told herself, she'd be calm too. "Alan, you can't tell me what to do. After all—"

"I am telling you," he countered easily. "I've come to the conclusion you've been asked too often in your life and not told often enough."

"Your conclusions don't interest me in the least," she shot back. "Who the hell are you to tell me anything?" For an answer, he pulled her closer. "I'm not going,"

Shelby began, experiencing what she realized must be desperation. "I have plans for the weekend. I'm—I'm leaving for the beach."

"Where's your coat?"

"Alan, I said—"

Spotting the light jacket hanging on the coatrack behind the counter, Alan slipped it off and handed it to her. "Do you want your purse?"

"Will you get it through your head that I am *not* going with you?"

He ignored her and plucked the shoulder bag from behind the counter. Taking the keys that lay beside it, he gripped Shelby's arm and pulled her through the rear of the shop.

"Dammit, Alan, I said I'm not going." Shelby found herself presumptuously shoved into the rain while Alan locked her back door. "I don't want to go anywhere with you."

"Too bad." He pocketed her keys, then slipped into his own coat while Shelby stood stubbornly in the downpour.

She swiped the dripping hair out of her eyes and planted her feet. "You can't make me."

He lifted a brow, taking a long, thoughtful study of her. She was livid and drenched and beautiful in her own fashion. And he noted, with satisfaction, just a little unsure of herself. It was about time. "We're going to have to start to keep count of how many times you tell me I can't," he commented before he grabbed her arm and dragged her to his car.

"If you think—" Shelby broke off as she was shoved, unceremoniously, inside. "If you think," she began again, "that I'm impressed by the caveman routine, you couldn't be more mistaken." It wasn't often that she was haughtily dignified, but when she put her mind to it, no one did it better than Shelby. Even soaking wet. "Give me back my keys." Imperiously she held out her hand, palm up.

Alan took it, pressed a lingering kiss to the center, then started the car.

Shelby curled her hand into a fist as if to subdue the warmth that started in her palm and shot out everywhere. "Alan, I don't know what's gotten into you, but it has to stop. Now, I want my keys so I can get back inside."

"After dinner," he said pleasantly and backed out of the alley. "How was your week?"

Shelby sat back and folded her arms. It wasn't until then that she realized she still had Alan's rainbow in her hand. She stuffed it in the pocket of the jacket that lay in a heap beside her, then flopped back again. "I'm not having dinner with you."

"I thought someplace quiet would be best." He turned right, keeping pace with the heavy, sluggish traffic. "You look a bit tired, love; haven't you been sleeping well?"

"I've been sleeping just fine," she lied. "I was out late last night." Deliberately she turned to him. "On a date."

Alan controlled the swift surge of jealousy. Her ability to push the right buttons to get under his skin was no longer a surprise. He met the simmering gray eyes briefly. "Have a good time?"

"I had a *marvelous* time. David's a musician, very sensitive. Very passionate," she added with relish. "I'm crazy about him." David might have been surprised, as he was engaged to one of Shelby's closest friends, but she doubted the subject would come up again. "As a matter of fact," she continued with sudden inspiration, "he's coming by to pick me up at seven. So, I'd appreciate it if you'd just turn around and take me home."

Instead of obliging as she hoped or raging as she expected, Alan glanced at his watch. "That's too bad. I doubt we'll be back by then." While Shelby sat in stony silence he pulled up to the curb. "Better put on your jacket; we'll have to walk half a block." When she neither moved nor spoke, he leaned across her as if to open the door. His mouth brushed over her ear. "Unless you'd like to stay in the car and neck."

Shelby turned her head, ready with a furious retort. She found her lips against his, lightly, devastatingly. In a quick move, she pushed out of her side of the car, whipping the jacket over her shoulders.

They'd play the scenario out, she told herself as she worked on leveling her breathing. And when she got back her keys, she was going to make him suffer for every minute of it. Alan joined her on the sidewalk, took her hands, and just looked at her. He felt her initial resistance melt before the time could be measured.

"You tasted of the rain," he murmured, before he gave in to the temptation to finish the promise of that brief meeting of lips, the press of bodies. The week of staying away from her had nearly driven him mad.

Rain pelted them, and Shelby thought of waterfalls. Her jacket slipped off her shoulders, and she thought of rainbows. All needs, all wishes, sped through her: sweet pangs of longing, half-formed dreams. How had she gone all her life without him when she could no longer keep sane for a week without being touched like this?

Reluctantly Alan drew her away. A moment longer, he knew, and he'd forget they were on a public street. Her face was pale ivory dashed with sweet spring rain. Drops clung to the lashes surrounding those pure gray eyes. They should be alone, he thought, in some gloomy evening forest or rain-splattered field. Then there'd be no drawing away. He slipped the jacket back over her shoulders.

"I like your hair wet." In a slow possessive move, he ran a hand through it. Without another word, he draped an arm around her and led her down the street.

Shelby knew the restaurant. All dim corners and smoky music. By ten o'clock that night, it would be noisy and jammed with people. A man like Alan would avoid it then, while she would seek it out. Now it was subdued—pale wooden floors, flickering candles, muted conversations.

"Good evening, Senator." The maître d' beamed over Alan before his gaze shifted to Shelby. He beamed again. "Nice to see you again, Ms. Campbell."

"Good evening, Mario," Shelby returned, searching for her hauteur.

"Your table's waiting." He guided them through to a back corner table where the candle was burned halfway down. There was enough Latin in Mario that he scented romance and appreciated it. "A bottle of wine?" he asked as he held Shelby's chair.

"*Pouilly Fuisse, Bichot,*" Alan told him without consulting Shelby.

"1979," Mario said with a nod of approval. "Your waiter will be with you shortly.

Shelby flipped her damp hair out of her eyes. "Maybe I want a beer."

"Next time," Alan agreed amiably.

"There isn't going to be a next time. I mean it, Alan," she said jerkily as he traced a line down the back of her hand with his fingertip. "I wouldn't be here if you hadn't locked me out of my house. Don't touch me that way," she added in a furious undertone.

"How would you like me to touch you? You have very sensitive hands," he murmured before she could answer. He grazed a thumb over her knuckle and felt the quick tremor. Tonight, he promised himself, he was going to feel that tremor again—at every pulse point. "How many times did you think of me this week?"

"I didn't think of you," Shelby tossed back, then felt a flash of guilt at the new lie. "All right, what if I did?" She attempted to snatch her hand away, but Alan merely slipped his fingers through hers and held it still. It was a simple, conventional gesture, one a civilized man could use in a public place without drawing eyes. Though she knew it, tried to scorn it, Shelby felt the pleasure ripple down to her toes. "I felt badly because I'd been nasty. After your behavior tonight, I only wish I'd been nastier. I can be," she added on a threat.

Alan only smiled as Mario brought the wine to the table. Watching Shelby, Alan tasted it, then nodded. "Very good. It's the sort of flavor that stays with you for hours. Later, when I kiss you, the taste will still be there."

The blood began to hum in her ears. "I'm only here because you dragged me."

To his credit, Mario didn't spill a drop of the wine he poured as he listened.

Her eyes heated as Alan continued to smile. "And since you refuse to give me my keys, I'll simply walk to the nearest phone and call a locksmith. *You'll* get the bill."

"After dinner," Alan suggested. "How do you like the wine?"

Scowling, Shelby lifted the glass and drained half the contents. "It's fine." Her eyes, insolent now, stayed level with his. "This isn't a date, you know."

"It's becoming more of a filibuster, isn't it? More wine?"

The patience was back. She wanted to pound her fists on the table in the teeth of it. That would set the tongues wagging, she thought, tempted. And serve him right. Then she thought of the chatty little article in the paper and ground her teeth instead. Shelby shrugged as he topped off her glass. "Wine and candlelight won't do you any good."

"No?" He decided against pointing out that she was holding his hand now as much as he was holding hers. "Well, I thought it was time for something more traditional."

"Really?" She had to smile. "Then, I should've gotten a box of chocolates or a bouquet of roses. *That's* traditional."

"I knew you'd rather have a rainbow."

"You know too damn much." She plucked up the menu the waiter set at her elbow and buried her face behind it. Since he'd dragged her out in the rain, she might as well eat. Stuff herself, Shelby corrected. Her appetite had returned in full force. So had her energy, she reluctantly admitted. The moment she'd seen him again, the listlessness had vanished.

"Are you ready to order, Ms. Campbell?"

Shelby glanced up at the waiter and aimed a smile. "Yes, I am. I'll have the seafood salad with avocado, the consommé, the loin of lamb with bearnaise sauce, a baked potato, and the artichoke hearts. I'll look at the pastry cart later."

The waiter scribbled, without flicking an eyebrow at the length of her order. "Senator?"

"The house salad," he said, grinning at Shelby's bland expression. "And the scampi. The walk in the rain gave you an appetite, I see."

"Since I'm here, I might as well choke down a few bites. Well..." In one of her lightning changes of moods, she rested her folded arms on the table and leaned over them. "We have to pass the time, don't we? What shall we talk about, Senator? How are things on the Hill?"

"Busy."

"Ah, the classic understatement. You've been working overtime to block Breiderman's bill. Well done, I'm forced to say. Then there's your current pet project. Any progress in squeezing out the Federal funds you need."

"There've been a few steps forward." He eyed her thoughtfully a moment. For a woman who had such an aversion to politics, she was well informed. "The mayor's enthusiastic about setting up the same kind of shelters here that we started in Boston. For now, we'll have to rely mostly on contributions and volunteers. We'll need a lot more before we can count on the support to set them up nationwide."

"You've got a long fight on your hands with the current financial picture and the budget cuts."

"I know. I'll win eventually." A smile touched his lips lightly. "I can be very patient up to a point, and then I can be very... insistent."

Not quite trusting the gleam in his eyes, Shelby remained silent as their salads were served. "You stepped on a few toes in Breiderman's case; they'll step back."

"That's the name of the game. Nothing worthwhile's ever without complications. I—" He filled her glass again. "Have a penchant for solving them as they come."

Not bothering to pretend she misunderstood him this time, Shelby speared a forkful of salad and ate it thoughtfully. "You can't organize a romance like a campaign, Senator. Particularly with someone who knows a great many of the moves."

"It is an interesting concept." Humor was in his eyes and around the edges of his slow, serious smile. Shelby found that her fingers were itching to touch his face. "You'll admit my statements have been clear. I haven't made any promises I won't keep, Shelby."

"I'm not one of your constituents."

"That doesn't change my platform."

Shelby shook her head, half-exasperated, half-amused. "I'm not going to argue with you on your turf." Toying with the remains of her salad, she glanced back up at him. "I suppose you saw the picture in the paper."

"Yes." It had bothered her, he realized, though she spoke lightly and with a trace of a smile. "I enjoyed being reminded of that particular moment. I'm sorry it upset you."

"It didn't," she said too quickly. On a faint sound of annoyance, she shook her head. "Not really." The waiter removed her salad and replaced it with consommé. Shelby began to stir it absently. "I suppose it just reminded me how much you're in the public eye. Does it ever bother you?"

"Off and on. Publicity's an intricate part of my profession. It can be a means to an end, or a basic nuisance." He wanted to see her smile. "Of course, I'm interested to get my father's reaction when he gets wind I was at the zoo with a Campbell."

The faint tension in her shoulders relaxed when she laughed. "Do you fear for your inheritance, Alan?"

"My skin more," he countered. "My hearing at the least. I expect to pick up the phone any day and be bellowed at."

She grinned as she picked up her wine. "Do you let him think he intimidates you?"

"From time to time. It keeps him happy."

Shelby picked up a roll, broke it in two, and offered half to Alan "If you were smart, you'd give me a very wide berth. You really shouldn't risk a broken eardrum: it makes it difficult to hear what the opposition's plotting in the next room."

"I can deal with my father—when the time comes."

Nibbling on the roll, she gave him a steady look. "Meaning after you've dealt with me."

He lifted his glass in a small toast. "Precisely."

"Alan." She smiled again, more confident after food and wine. "You're not going to deal with me."

"We'll have to see, won't we?" he said easily. "Here's your lamb."

Chapter Seven

Shelby might have wished she hadn't enjoyed herself quite so much. She might have wished Alan hadn't been able to make her laugh quite so easily. Or that he hadn't been able to charm her into walking down M Street in the rain to window-shop and people-watch—and to have one last glass of wine at a crowded little café.

Shelby might have wished it, but she didn't. For the first time in a week, she could laugh and relax and enjoy without effort. There'd be consequences—there were always consequences. She'd think about them tomorrow.

More than once someone breezed by their table with a greeting for Shelby and a speculative look at Alan. It reminded her that smoky little clubs were her territory. Ballet openings were his. That was something else she'd think about tomorrow.

"Hello, gorgeous."

Shelby glanced up and around as hands dropped onto her shoulders. "Hello, David. Hi, Wendy."

"Hey, you were supposed to give us a call tonight," David reminded her. The piano player switched to something hot and pulsing. David glanced over automatically. "We caught the new play at Ford's without you."

Wendy, soft and graceful with hair rippling past her waist, grinned as she slipped an arm around David's waist. "You didn't miss anything."

"I got..." Shelby cast a glance at Alan. "Sidetracked. Alan, David and Wendy."

"Nice to meet you." Alan gave the gangly man with the wisp of beard a slow smile. "Would you like to join us?"

"Thanks, but we're just heading out." David ruffled Shelby's hair before he snitched her wine for a quick sip. "Got to play at a wedding tomorrow."

"David's still trying to figure out how he can play at ours next month. Hey, I've got to call you later about that Greek caterer you told me about." Wendy sent Alan a friendly grin. "Shelby says ouzo livens up a reception. Listen, we'll see you later," she added as she tugged on David's arm.

Alan watched them skirt around tables on their way to the door. "He works fast," Alan commented as he lifted his wine.

"David?" Shelby sent him a puzzled look. "Actually his fastest speed is crawl unless he's got a guitar in his hands."

"Really?" Alan's eyes met hers as he sipped, but she didn't understand the amusement in them. "You only stood him up tonight, and already he's planning his wedding to someone else."

"Stood him—" she began on a laugh, then remembered. "Oh." Torn between annoyance and her own sense of the ridiculous, Shelby toyed with the stem of her glass. "Men are fickle creatures," she decided.

"Apparently." Reaching over, he lifted her chin with a fingertip. "You're holding up well."

"I don't like to wear my heart on my sleeve." Exasperated, amused, she muffled a laugh. "Dammit, he would have to pick tonight to show up here."

"Of all the gin joints in all the towns..."

This time the laugh escaped fully. "Well done," Shelby told him. "I should've thought of that line myself; I heard the movie not long ago."

"Heard it?"

"*Mmm-hmm.* Well . . ." She lifted her glass in a toast. "To broken hearts?"

"Or foolish lies?" Alan countered.

Shelby wrinkled her nose as she tapped her glass against his. "I usually tell very good ones. Besides, I *did* date David. Once. Three years ago." She finished off her wine. "Maybe four. You can stop grinning in that smug, masculine way any time, Senator."

"Was I?" Rising, he offered Shelby her damp jacket. "How rude of me."

"It would've been more polite not to acknowledge that you'd caught me in a lie," she commented as they worked their way through the crowd and back into the rain. "Which you wouldn't have done if you hadn't made me so mad that I couldn't think of a handier name to give you in the first place."

"If I work my way through the morass of that sentence it seems to be my fault." Alan slipped an arm around her shoulders in so casually friendly a manner she didn't protest. "Suppose I apologize for not giving you time to think of a lie that would hold up?"

"It seems fair." Shelby lifted her face to the rain, forgetting how she had cursed it only hours before. It was soft and cool and clean on her skin. She could have walked in it for hours. "But I'm not going to thank you for dinner," she added with a flash of laughter in her eyes. She turned, leaning back against the door of his car when they reached it. "Or the wine and the candlelight."

Alan looked into the insolent, rain-washed face and wanted her, desperately. She'd bring touches of that insolence to her passion, and touches of the freshness. He dipped his hands into his pockets before he could give in to the urge to pull her to him then and there. "How about the rainbow?"

A smile tilted the corners of her mouth. "Maybe I'll thank you for that. I haven't decided." Quickly she slipped into the car. Her knees had gone weak, she'd discovered, with that one long look he'd given her before he'd spoken. It would be wise to keep the mood as light as it had been in the café—at least until she was safely inside her apartment and he was safely out. "You know," she went on as Alan slid behind the wheel, "I was planning to drive to the beach tonight. You mucked up my plans."

"Do you like the beach in the rain?"

"It might not have been raining there," Shelby pointed out while the engine purred. "And anyway I do."

"I like it best in a storm." Alan steered the Mercedes around a corner. "At dusk—when there's just enough light to watch the sky and the water churn."

"Really?" Intrigued, she studied his profile. "I would have thought you'd prefer quiet winter beaches where you could take long walks and think deep thoughts."

"Everything in its time," Alan murmured.

She could see it—the lightning, the thunder, the breath of windy excitement. Something more than wine warmed her blood. Undercurrents. She'd known there were undercurrents in him from the first moment she'd seen him, but now they seemed closer to the surface. There'd be a time, if she wasn't careful, when they'd simply sweep her away.

"My sister lives in Atlantic City," Alan said casually. "I like to shoot up there at odd times during the off-season to spend a couple of days at the beach and lose money in her casino."

"Your sister owns a casino?" Shelby turned back to him again.

"She's partners with her husband in a couple of them." Amused by the surprise in Shelby's voice, he sent her a quick grin. "Rena used to deal blackjack. Still does occasionally. Did you consider that my family would be very staid, very proper, and very dull, Shelby?"

"Not precisely," she answered, though she had for the most part. "At least not from what I've heard about your father. Myra seems very fond of him."

"They like to argue with each other. He's every bit as opinionated as she is."

He parked beside her building, then got out before Shelby could tell him not to bother to see her to the door. "You've gotten your share of dunkings tonight, Senator." As they climbed the stairs she automatically reached into her purse for her keys.

"I still have them," Alan reminded her as he drew them out of his pocket. Watching her, he jiggled them in his palm. "They should be worth a cup of coffee."

Shelby frowned at him. "I think that's bribery."

"Bribery?" His stare was mild and reasonable. "No, it was a supposition."

Shelby hesitated, then sighed. She understood him well enough by now to know that they could end up debating his supposition for an hour on the landing. And he'd still end up with his cup of coffee. Stepping aside, she gestured for him to unlock the door. "Coffee," she said as though stating the boundary lines. After she stripped out of her jacket, Shelby tossed it carelessly over a kitchen chair. The cat struggled out from under it, leapt to the floor, and glared out of his good eye. "Oh, sorry." Shelby poked into a cabinet and came out with an envelope of cat food. "It's his fault," she told Moshe. As the cat attacked his meal Shelby looked back at Alan. "He doesn't appreciate it when I'm late with his dinner. He's very regimented."

Alan gave the plump, greedy cat a cursory glance. "He doesn't appear deprived."

"No." Tossing her bangs out of her eyes, Shelby turned to the sink to fill the percolator. "But he's easily annoyed. If I—" She lost her train of thought when Alan's hands descended to her shoulders. "If I forget to feed him, he—" The percolator clattered into the sink as Alan's mouth grazed her ear. "Sulks," she finished, switching off the tap with a jerk. "Roommates who sulk," she managed in an abruptly thready voice as she set the percolator on the counter, "make things difficult."

"I imagine," Alan murmured. Brushing the hair away from the nape of her neck, he nibbled on the sensitive skin. Shelby felt the fire start and fought to get the plug into the wall socket. "Shelby..." His hands skimmed down her sides to rest at her waist.

She was going to ignore it, she told herself. Absolutely ignore what he was doing to her. "What?"

"Mmm." Alan trailed his lips around the side of her neck. Her scent was more vibrant there, he discovered, just there above the collarbone. He skimmed his tongue over it and listened to her quick, unsteady inhalation of breath. "You didn't put any coffee in the pot."

She shivered, then gripped the counter with both hands to keep it from happening again. "What?"

Alan reached around her to pull the plug out. "You didn't," he began and turned her to face him, "put any coffee in." He brushed a kiss at one corner of her mouth, then just as lightly, at the other.

For a moment, she weakened, closing her eyes. "In where?"

His lips curved against her cheekbone. "In the percolator."

"It'll perk in a minute," she murmured when his lips skimmed over her eyelids. She heard him laugh softly and wondered why it sounded triumphant. It took all her effort to fight off the brushfire that was already getting out of control. "Alan..." Featherlight kisses trailed over her face, adding fuel to the blaze. "You're trying to seduce me."

"No, I'm not." He nipped gently at her lips, then left them unsatisfied as he journeyed to her throat. He wanted to feel that desperately pounding pulse. "I *am* seducing you."

"No." Shelby lifted her hands to his chest to push him away. Somehow they crept up around his neck. "We're not going to make love."

Alan barely controlled the urgent flare of need as his fingers wound their way into her hair. "No?" He teased her lips again. "Why?"

"Because..." She fought to remember who she was. Where she was. "Because it's...the road to perdition?"

He gave a muffled laugh against her mouth before his tongue slipped in to tempt her. "Try again."

"Because..." It was building too quickly, beyond what she understood. Needs weren't supposed to be so painful. Hunger wasn't supposed to come in waves that enervated you. She knew that because she'd felt both before. This had to be something different, and yet it seemed to have no name at all. There was weakness, such weakness, and a driving, burning force that threatened to consume everything she thought she knew. "No." Panic, sharp and real, broke through. "No, I want you too much. I can't let this happen, don't you see?"

"Too late." Still roaming her face with kisses, he guided her through the apartment. "Much too late, Shelby." He slipped the blouse from her shoulders and let it float to the floor. This time, the first time, he thought, it would be a seduction. One that both of them would remember in all the years to come. "Soft," he murmured, "much too soft to resist." Taking his time, he trailed his hands up her arms, over her shoulders. "Do you know how often I've thought of being with you like this? How often I've thought of touching you—" his fingers brushed over the thin camisole to stroke her breast "—like this." Without a sound, her skirt dropped to the floor at the doorway to the bedroom. "Do you hear the rain, Shelby?"

She felt the bedspread brush her shoulders as they eased onto the bed. "Yes."

"I'm going to make love with you." His lips were at her ear again, destroying even the pretense of refusal. "And every time you hear the rain, you'll remember."

She wouldn't need the rain to remember, Shelby thought. Had her heart ever beat so fast? Had her skin ever seemed so soft? Yes, she could hear the rain, drumming and drumming on the roof, against the window-pane. But she wouldn't need to hear the sound of it again to remember the way his mouth fit so perfectly against hers, the way her body seemed to mold itself to the lines of his. She would only have to think of him to remember the way the rain-dampened freshness clung to his hair or the way the sound of her name came in a whisper through his lips.

She'd never given the gift of her pliancy to a man before, though she wasn't aware of it. Now, she yielded, letting him guide her where she'd been so reluctant—or so afraid—to go. To mindlessness.

He seemed to want to touch, to taste, all of her, but so slowly, so thoroughly, she could float, insubstantial as a mist, on feelings alone. With only fingertips, with only lips, he aroused her to a plane of contentment that was irresistible.

Shelby hadn't understood true languor until she reached for the buttons of his shirt. Her arms were so heavy. Her hands, always so clever, her fingers always so deft, fumbled, drawing out the process and unwittingly driving him to desperation.

His mouth grew suddenly greedy on hers, his body pressing down to trap her hands between them. Perhaps it was that unconscious show of dominance, or perhaps it was the overload of suppressed needs, but she ceased to yield against him and began to take.

Her hunger matched his, and when it threatened to surpass him, his built to balance it again. Shelby found those strong, subtle muscles, freed of the shirt, but her hands no longer fumbled. It seemed like a race, who could drive whom further, and faster. His mouth sped down her, lingering at points of pleasure she hadn't known existed until he found them, exploited them, then moved on. He drew the bare swathe of silk down, and further down, though his caresses had ceased to be gentle. Neither of them looked for gentleness. What was between them had ignited at the first meeting and had simmered too long.

Alan felt her tremble wherever he touched, wherever his tongue flicked over her skin. He knew she'd left fear far behind. This was the passion, the pure, undiluted passion he'd known she would give to him if he waited for her. It was the whirlwind he'd needed, and the whirlwind she brought.

Aggressive, all fire, all flash, she moved with him, against him, for him, until his control was ripped apart—

shredded and forgotten. He could taste her with each breath he drew into his lungs—everything wild and sweet and tempting.

Neither was leading now, but both were led. Shelby took him into her on a cry that was muffled against his mouth and had nothing to do with surrender. Thunder and lightning, they fed each other.

The rain still fell. The sound was no softer, no louder. They might have lain together for hours or for moments. Neither had any thought of time, only of place. Here.

Shelby curled into Alan, eyes closed, breathing steady at last, her mind and body so peaceful the storm might never have taken place. But it had been the storm, her part in it, her yielding to it, that had given her the serenity she hadn't even known she craved. Alan—Alan was her peace, her heart, her home.

Steady, solid, whimsical, persistent. There were too many labels for him—perhaps that was why she was drawn to him again and again, and why she'd continued to step away.

Alan shifted, drawing her closer. He could still feel the ripples: excitement, passion, emotions too vibrant to name. Shelby continued to pour through him like a heady, breathtaking wind that blew in all directions at once. Brisk or sultry, she was a breeze that whisked away the harshness of the world he knew too much about. He needed that kind of magic from her, the same way he needed to give her whatever it was in him she was drawn to.

Lazily . . . possessively he ran a hand down her back.

"*Mmm*, again," Shelby murmured.

With a quiet laugh, Alan stroked up and down until she was ready to purr. "Shelby . . ." She gave another sigh as an answer and snuggled closer. "Shelby, there's something warm and fluffy under my feet."

"Mm-hmm."

"If it's your cat, he's not breathing."

"MacGregor."

He kissed the top of her head. "What?"

She gave a muffled laugh against his shoulder. "MacGregor," she repeated. "My pig."

There was silence for a moment while he tried to digest this. "I beg your pardon?"

The dry serious tone had more laughter bubbling up. Would she ever be able to face a day without hearing it? "Oh, say that again. I love it." Because she had to see his face, Shelby found the energy to lean across him and grope for the matches on the nightstand. Skin rubbed distractingly against skin while she struck one and lit a candle. "MacGregor," she said, giving Alan a quick kiss before she gestured to the foot of the bed.

Alan studied the smiling porcine face. "You named a stuffed purple pig after me?"

"Alan, is that any way to talk about our child?" His eyes shifted to hers in an expression so masculine and ironic, she collapsed on his chest in a fit of giggles. "I put him there because he was supposed to be the only MacGregor who charmed his way into my bed."

"Really." Alan tugged on her hair until she lifted her face, full of amusement and fun, to his. "Is that what I did?"

"You knew damn well I wouldn't be able to resist balloons and rainbows forever." The candlelight flickered over his face. Shelby traced the shifting light with a fingertip. "I meant to resist your charms; I really did. I wasn't going to do this."

Alan took her wrist, guiding her hand over so that he could press a kiss to the palm. "Make love with me?"

"No." Shelby's gaze traveled from his mouth to his eyes. "Be in love with you."

She felt his fingers tighten on her wrist, then loosen slowly as his eyes stayed dark and fixed on hers. Beneath her, she felt the change in his heartbeat. "And are you?"

"Yes." The word, hardly audible, thundered in his head.

Alan brought her to him, cradling her head against his chest, feeling her low slow expulsion of air as his arm came around her. He hadn't expected her to give him so much so soon. "When?"

"When?" Shelby repeated, enjoying the solid feel of his chest under her cheek. "Sometime between when we first stepped out on the Writes' terrace and when I opened a basket of strawberries."

"It took you that long? All I had to do was look at you."

Shelby brought her head up and found her eyes locked with his. He wouldn't exaggerate, she knew. It wasn't his style. Simple words with simple truth. Overwhelmed, she framed his face in her hands. "If you had told me that a week ago, a day ago, I would have thought you were mad." On a flow of laughter, she pressed her mouth to his. "Maybe you are—it doesn't seem to matter." With a sigh, she melted against him. "It doesn't seem to matter at all."

She knew she had tenderness in her—for children and small animals. She'd never felt real tenderness for a man. But when she kissed him now, with words of love still echoing in her head, Shelby was swamped with it. Her hands came back to his face, her artist's fingers tracing, molding the shape until she thought she knew it well enough to conjure it out of air if someone asked her to.

Then she trailed them down, over the column of his throat, along the shoulders firm with muscle. Shoulders to depend on—strong enough to hold your problems if you needed them to. But she wouldn't ask; it was enough to know they were there. With her mouth still tasting, still lingering on his, she ran her fingers down his arms as if in the first storm of lovemaking she'd been too frantic to really see the whole man. She realized as she nuzzled into his neck that she could smell herself on him, and thought it was wonderful. His arms came around her and they stayed just so for a moment—naked, entwined, content.

"Can I tell you something without it going to your head?" Shelby murmured as she ran her fingers down his chest, over his ribs.

"Probably not." His voice had thickened from the pleasure of being touched. "I'm easily flattered."

"In my workroom..." Shelby pressed her lips to his chest and felt his heartbeat thud faster against them. "When I messed up your shirt and you took it off to rinse it? I turned around and saw you—I wanted to get my hands on you like this." She ran her palms up, then down again to where his waist narrowed. "Just like this, I nearly did."

Alan felt his blood start to pound—in his head, his heart, his loins. "I wouldn't have put up much of a fight."

"If I'd decided to have you, Senator," she murmured on a sultry laugh, "you wouldn't have had a chance."

"Is that so?"

Shelby ran her tongue down his rib cage. *"Mmm,"* she said when she heard the small, quick intake of breath. "Just so. A MacGregor will always buckle under to a Campbell."

Alan started to form a retort, then her fingers skimmed his thigh. As a politician, he knew the value of a debate—but sometimes they didn't require words. She could have the floor first.

He could float under the strong, skilled touch of her hands. As the need built in power, so did the pleasure of the prolonging. She seemed absorbed with the shape of his body, the texture of his skin. The candlelight flickered, pale red, against the back of his eyelids as he lay steeped in what she brought him. The rain continued its monotonous song, but he began to hear only Shelby's quiet sighs and murmurs.

She moved slowly, loitering here, nibbling there. A touch could weaken or excite. A kiss could soothe or madden. His pulse beat faster, then faster still, until he knew it was time to present his side. In a swift move, he rolled her beneath him.

Her face was flushed with heat, her breathing unsteady with the edges of passion just begun. Alan looked at her, wanting this memory for cold nights and listless afternoons.

The wild splash of red that was her hair tumbled over the vivid green of the bedspread. Shadows from the candle shifted over her face, reminding him of the impression he'd first had of her—the gypsy—open fires, weeping violins. Her eyes were dark, pure gray, and waiting.

"We MacGregors," he murmured, "have ways of... dealing with Campbells."

His mouth lowered but paused a whisper from hers. He saw that her lids had fluttered down yet hadn't closed. She watched him through her lashes while her breath came quickly. Slowly he shifted his head to nibble along her jawline.

Shelby closed her eyes on a moan that was as much in protest as appreciation. Her lips were aching for his, but the feel of that clever mouth teasing over her skin brought such quick, such vibrant, thrills. His hands were already on her, moving with a thoroughness she knew he would always bring to her.

Lazy, lengthy, devastating circles were traced around her breasts with tongue and teeth and lips; however, he didn't allow her to concentrate on only the sensation there. His fingers skimmed low over her stomach, taunting, promising, until she arched against him, desperate for that blinding flash of heat. But he was in no hurry now and so drew out her pleasure; built her needs layer by layer with that intense patience that left her helpless.

His mouth inched lower, his tongue flicking fires, his hand fanning them. Neither knew the moment when the world ceased to exist. It might have been winked out in an instant; it might have spun slowly to a stop. But there was nothing but them, flesh against flesh, sigh for sigh, need for need.

His mouth came back to hers, drawing out that last moment before oblivion would claim them. She was trembling when he slipped inside her, harnessing the power rushing through him. He would pleasure her until they were both mad from it. He took her slowly, listening to the deep, shuddering breaths that mixed with his as their lips clung, drinking in the hot, moist tastes of her mouth.

Time seemed to hold for them, then it came spinning back until it was all speed, all whirling urgency. Alan buried his face at her throat and went with the madness.

Chapter Eight

Dingy gloomy mornings tended to make Shelby pull the covers over her head and tune out for an extra hour after her mental alarm rang. This morning, feeling the warmth of Alan beside her, she snuggled closer and prepared to do the same thing. It was obvious, after his hand slid down her back and intimately over her bottom, that he had other plans.

"Are you awake?" he murmured next to her ear. "Or should I wake you?"

She gave him an *mmm* for an answer.

"I take that to mean you're undecided." Alan moved his lips down to her throat where her pulse beat slow and steady. How long, he wondered idly, would it take him to change that? "Maybe I can influence you to take a firmer stand."

Slowly, enjoying her drowsy response, he began to kiss and fondle. It seemed impossible, he knew, that he could have steeped himself in her the night before and still want her so feverishly this morning. But her skin was so warm and soft—so was her mouth. Her movements beneath him remained lazy but not sluggish. He felt, as he wanted to, the gradual increase of her pulse.

Passion slept in her so that she seemed content to let him touch and explore as he chose while she aroused him with her sighs alone. The morning grew late—but they had forever.

Their lovemaking had a misty, dreamy aura that lasted from the first casual touch to the last breathless kiss.

"I think," Shelby said as Alan nuzzled lazily between her breasts, "that we should stay in bed until it stops raining."

"Too soon," he murmured. "You should have thought of that days ago." With his eyes closed, he could see her lying sleepily beneath him, her skin still heated from his. "Are you going to open the shop today?"

She yawned, running her hands along the ridge of muscles in his upper back. "Kyle takes care of it on Saturdays. We can stay right here and sleep."

He kissed the curve of her breasts, then slowly worked up to her throat. "I've a luncheon meeting this afternoon and some paperwork that has to be taken care of before Monday."

Of course, she thought, biting back a sigh. To a man like Alan, Saturday was just another day of the week. A glance at the clock showed her it was barely seven. In reflex, she curled into him. Time was already slipping away. "That gives us a few hours to stay right here."

"What about breakfast?"

Shelby considered for a minute, then decided she was lazier than she was hungry. "Can you cook?"

"No."

Drawing her brows together, she grabbed both of his ears and drew his head up. "Not at all? That's remarkably chauvinistic for a man whose policies primarily reflect the feminist viewpoint."

Alan lifted a brow. "I don't expect you to be able to cook either." Amusement shot into his eyes. "Can you?"

Shelby struggled with a grin. "Barely."

"I find that odd for someone with your appetite."

"I eat out a lot. What about you?"

"McGee sees to it."

"McGee?"

"He's what you might term a family retainer." Alan twined a tumbled curl around his finger. "He was our butler when I was a boy, and when I moved to D.C., he insisted, in his stoic, unmovable way, on coming with me." He gave her the quick flash of grin that came rarely to him. "I've always been his favorite."

"Is that so?" Lazily Shelby folded her arms behind her head. She could picture him as a boy, seeing beyond what other boys saw and storing it. "Why?"

"If I weren't modest, I'd confess that I was always a well-mannered, even-tempered child who never gave my parents a moment's trouble."

"Liar," she said easily. "How'd you get the broken nose?"

The grin became rueful. "Rena punched me."

"Your sister broke your nose?" Shelby burst out with delighted and unsympathetic laughter. "The blackjack dealer, right? Oh, I love it!"

Alan caught Shelby's nose between two fingers and gave it a quick twist. "It was rather painful at the time."

"I imagine." She kept right on laughing as he shifted to her side. "Did she make a habit of beating you up?"

"She didn't beat me up," he corrected with some dignity. "She was trying to beat Caine up because he'd teased her about making calf's eyes at one of his friends."

"Typical brotherly intimidation."

"In any event," Alan put in mildly, "I went to drag her off him, she took another swing, missed him, and hit me. A full-power roundhouse, as I remember. That's when," he continued as Shelby gave another peal of laughter, "I decided against being a diplomat. It's always the neutral party that gets punched in the face."

"I'm sure . . ." Shelby dropped her head on his shoulder. "I'm sure she was sorry."

"Initially. But as I recall, after I'd stopped bleeding and threatening to kill both her and Caine, her reaction was a great deal like yours."

"Insensitive." Shelby ran apologetic kisses over his face. "Poor baby. Tell you what, I'll do penance and see about fixing you breakfast." With a quick burst of energy, she gave him a last kiss and bounded from the bed. "Come on, let's see what's in the kitchen." Finding a robe that had been tossed over a chair, Shelby waited until Alan slipped into his slacks. "You can make the coffee," she told him, "while I see if there's anything edible in the fridge."

"Sounds promising," Alan murmured.

"Now, don't get snotty before you know what might turn up," she advised. They passed through the living room where the cat simply rolled over on the sofa and ignored them. "He's still sulking," Shelby stated with a sigh. "Now I'll have to buy him chicken livers or something." She stopped to pull the water dish out of Auntie Em's cage. "He's a moody creature, isn't he?" she said to the bird. Auntie Em gave one impatient squawk, the extent of her vocabulary.

"Sounds like she got up on the wrong side of the perch," Alan commented.

"Oh, no. She's in a good mood if she says anything."

He gave Shelby an interested glance. "Did she?"

For an answer, she handed him the water bowl. "Here, you can take care of this before you start the coffee." Without waiting for an assent, she went through the kitchen to the side door to bring in the paper. Alan looked down at the container like a man who'd been handed a small damp-bottomed child. "It seems the President's

Mideast tour is still the top story," she noted before she tossed the paper onto the counter. "Do you like to travel?"

Recognizing the meaning behind the query, Alan switched off the water before he answered. "At times I enjoy it. At times it's simply a necessity. It isn't always possible to choose when and where I go."

Deliberately she shook off the mood. "I suppose not." Shelby opened the refrigerator and stared inside until she heard him move away to see to the bird. *Don't think about it,* she ordered herself fiercely. *You're not to think about it today.*

"Well," she began brightly when Alan came back into the room. "What we have here is a quart of milk, a couple of leftover cartons of Chinese, a very small slice of goat cheese, half a pack of Fig Newtons, and an egg."

Alan came up to look over her shoulder. "One egg?"

"All right, just wait a minute," Shelby told him while she nibbled on her lower lip. "You have to consider the possibilities."

"We could consider the restaurant around the corner."

"The man has no vision," Shelby muttered as she concentrated. "Let me see..." Moving aside, she rummaged through a cupboard. "Okay, I have...three, four, five slices of bread, if you count the heels. French toast." She smiled triumphantly. "That's two and a half pieces for each of us."

Alan nodded. "All right, you take the heels."

"Picky." Clucking her tongue, Shelby went back for the milk and the egg.

"Discriminating," he corrected, and left her to her creation while he made coffee.

For a few moments, they worked in companionable silence: Alan measured out coffee and water; Shelby dumped what she thought might be the right amount of milk into a bowl. Alan watched her rummage through a cupboard, pushing aside an empty jar, a large plastic container without a lid, and a loose-leaf notebook. "So there's where that is," she was muttering until she came up with a frying pan. As she rose Shelby caught his eye and the gleam of amusement.

"I don't do a great deal of this." Shelby put the pan on a burner and flicked on the flame.

"I'd remind you of that restaurant around the corner except..." His gaze flicked over the robe that dipped deep at her breasts and skimmed her thighs. "You'd have to get dressed."

Shelby smiled, a slow invitation, but when he took a step toward her, she dunked bread into the batter. "Get a plate."

He reached into the cupboard she indicated, then drew two plates out before he came to stand behind her. Leaning over, he brushed his lips below her ear, pleased with the quick tremor of response.

"The ones I burn," Shelby warned, "are all yours."

He chuckled and set the plates beside the stove. "Got any powdered sugar?"

"For what?" Catching her tongue between her teeth, Shelby flipped the bread over.

"For that." Alan opened three likely drawers before he located the flatware.

Rubbing her nose with the back of her hand, she glanced over as the last piece began to simmer in the pan. "Don't you use syrup?"

"No."

With a careless shrug, she slipped the last slice of toast onto a plate. "Well, you do today. I probably have some in...the second cabinet to the left," she decided. While he looked she meticulously divided one piece in half. Shelby had poured the coffee and brought the plates and cups to the table before he managed to locate the bottle.

"It looks like we have about a tablespoon," Alan decided as he tilted the bottle to its side.

"That's one and a half spoonfuls apiece." Sitting, Shelby held out her hand for the bottle. After pouring carefully, she passed the syrup back to him. "I have a hard time remembering what I'm nearly out of," she told him as she began to eat.

He fought to squeeze out the last drops from the bottle. "You must have six boxes of cat food in that cupboard."

"Moshe gets cranky if I don't keep a variety."

After tasting his breakfast, Alan found it better than he had expected. "I have a hard time understanding anyone as strong-willed as you being intimidated by a temperamental cat."

Shelby lifted her shoulders and continued to eat. "We all have our weaknesses. Besides, as roommates go, he's perfect. He doesn't listen in on my phone calls or borrow my clothes."

"Are those your prerequisites?"

"They're certainly in the top ten."

Watching her, Alan nodded. She'd plowed her way through the toast in record time. "If I promised to restrain myself from doing either of those things, would you marry me?"

The cup she had lifted froze halfway to her lips. For the first time since he'd met her, Alan saw Shelby totally and completely stunned. She put the coffee down untasted, then stared at it while hundreds of thoughts raced through her head. Dominating them all was the simple and basic emotion of fear.

"Shelby?"

Quickly she shook her head. She rose, clattering the flatware onto her plate and scooping it up to take it to the sink. She didn't speak—didn't dare speak yet. What threatened to come out was *yes,* and she feared that most of all. There was a pressure in her chest, a weight, a pain. It reminded her to let out the breath she'd been holding. As she did Shelby leaned heavily against the sink and stared into the rain. When Alan's hands came to her shoulders, she closed her eyes.

Why hadn't she been prepared? She knew that for a man like Alan love would lead to marriage. And marriage to children, she told herself as she tried to calm her nerves. If it wasn't what she wanted as well, she wouldn't feel this frenzied urge to say yes, and to say yes quickly. But it wasn't as simple as love to marriage to children, not with Alan. There was the Senator in front of his name, and that wouldn't be the highest title he'd attempt.

"Shelby." His voice was still gentle, though she thought she could feel tiny pulses of impatience and frustration in the fingers that moved on her shoulders. "I love you. You're the only woman I've ever wanted to spend my life with. I need mornings like this—waking with you."

"So do I."

He turned her to face him. The intensity was back in his eyes, that dark seriousness that had first attracted her to him. He scanned her face, slowly, thoroughly. "Then, marry me."

"You make it sound so simple—"

"No," he interrupted. "Not simple. Necessary, vital, but not simple."

"Don't ask me now." Shelby wrapped her arms around him and held him close. "Please don't. We're together, and I love you. Let that be enough for now."

He wanted to press. Instinct told him he had only to demand an answer to hear the one he needed. And yet...
He'd seen vulnerability when he'd looked into her face.
He'd seen a plea in her eyes—two things rare in Shelby Campbell. Two things that made it impossible for him to demand anything.

"I'll want you just as much tomorrow," he murmured, stroking her hair. "And a year from tomorrow. I can promise to wait to ask you again, Shelby, but I can't promise to wait until you're ready to answer."

"You don't have to promise." Tilting back her head, she put a hand on either side of his face. "You don't have to give me any promises. For now, let's just enjoy what we have—a rainy weekend with each other. We don't need to think about tomorrows, Alan, when we have so much today. Questions are for later." When she pressed her mouth to his, Shelby felt a wave of love so intense, it brought shivers of fear to her skin. "Come back to bed. Make love with me again. When you do, there's nothing and no one but you and me."

He felt her desperation, though he didn't fully understand it. Without a word, Alan picked her up and carried her back to bed.

"I can still send my regrets," Alan stated as he pulled the car up in front of his house.

"Alan, I don't mind going, really." Shelby leaned over to give him a quick kiss before she slid out of the car. The rain had slowed to a drizzling evening mist that dampened the shoulders of her short velvet jacket. "Besides, these dinner dances can be fun—even when they're disguised political functions."

Alan joined her on the sidewalk to tilt her chin for another kiss. "I believe you'd go anywhere as long as food was on the bill."

"It is an incentive all its own." Hooking an arm through his, Shelby started up the walk. "And I also get the opportunity of poking around your house while you're changing."

"You might find it a bit . . . sedate for your tastes."

With a smoky laugh, Shelby bit his ear. "You're not."

"I think," Alan considered as he opened the front door, "we'd have a more stimulating evening at home."

"I could be persuaded." After stepping inside, Shelby turned to wind her arms around his neck. "If you'd like to make the effort."

Before Alan could oblige, he heard a stiff little cough. McGee stood near the parlor doors, sturdy as a tree. His long lined face was expressionless. Over the distance of six feet, Alan felt the waves of disapproval. He nearly sighed. McGee could still stand like the perfectly mannered servant and throw off vibrations like a stern uncle. Since he'd been sixteen, Alan had had to deal with that dignified disapproval whenever he'd come home late or not in the most sober of conditions.

"You had several calls, Senator."

Alan's mouth nearly twitched before he controlled it. The *senator* was reserved for use in the presence of company. "Anything urgent, McGee?"

"Nothing urgent, Senator," he replied, rolling the *r* for emphasis and delighting Shelby.

"I'll see to them later, then. Shelby, this is McGee. He's been with my family since I was a boy."

"Hello, McGee." With no self-consciousness, Shelby released Alan to walk to his servant and offer her hand. "Are you a Highlander?"

"Ma'am. From Perthshire."

Her smile would have charmed the bark off any tree, even such a gnarled one. "My grandfather came from Dalmally. Do you know it?"

"Aye." Alan watched the faded eyes warm. "It's country worth seeing twice."

"I thought so myself, though I haven't been since I was seven. It's the mountains I remember most. Do you go back often?"

"Every spring to see the heather blooming. There's nothing like walking in the heather in June."

It was the longest, and Alan mused, the most romantic statement he had ever heard McGee make in the presence of anyone who wasn't family. Yet it didn't surprise him. "McGee, if you'll make some tea, I'll go up and change. Perhaps you could serve Ms. Campbell in the parlor."

"Campbell?" McGee's habitual stone face cracked with surprise as he stared from Alan to Shelby. "Campbell..." Briefly, very briefly, Shelby thought she caught a look of unholy glee in his eyes. "There's going t'be a ruckus," he murmured before turning on his heel to stride toward the kitchen.

"Not everyone would have gotten that much out of him," Alan commented as he steered Shelby into the parlor.

"Was that a lot?"

"My love, for McGee, that was an oratory."

"*Hmm,* well, I liked him," Shelby decided as she wandered through the room. "Especially the way he scolded you, without saying a word, for staying out all night."

Slipping her hands into the deep pockets of her slim skirt, she studied the seascape on the wall. The room was ordered, calm, with subtle touches of turbulence. It suited the man, she mused. Shelby remembered the jade krater she'd made the day after she'd met him. He'd have to have it for this room, she reflected. Strange that she should have made something then that fit so perfectly into his world. Why couldn't she?

Forcing the thought back, she turned around to smile at him. "I like how you live."

The simple statement surprised him. Simple statements weren't the norm for Shelby. He'd expected some light-hearted comment with a slick double edge. Going to her, Alan ran his hands up the arms of her jacket, still damp from the drizzle. "I like seeing you here."

She wanted to cling to him then, right then, desperately. If only he could tell her everything would always be as it was at that moment—that nothing would change or interfere... Instead she touched a palm to his cheek and kept her voice light. "You'd better go up and change, Senator. The sooner we get there—" now she grinned "—the sooner we can get away."

He pressed her palm to his lips. "I like your thought process. I won't be long."

Alone, Shelby closed her eyes and gave in to the panic. What was she going to do? How could she love him, need him, like this when her head was screaming with warnings. *Don't. Be careful. Remember.*

There were a dozen solid, viable reasons why they didn't belong together. She could list them all ... when he wasn't looking at her. She didn't even need that shivery misty fear that she kept trapped in the back of her mind.

She looked at the room again, closely. There was a basic order here, a style she admired, the understated wealth she understood. Fastidiousness without fussiness. But it wasn't *her* style. Shelby lived in chaos not because she was too lazy or too indifferent to order her life, but because she *chose* chaos.

There was an innate goodness in Alan she wasn't sure she had. A tolerance she was sure she didn't. Alan ran on facts or theories that had been well thought-out. She ran on imagination and possibilities. It was crazy, Shelby told herself as she dragged a hand through her hair. How could two people with so little common ground love each other so much?

She should have run, she told herself. She should have run fast and far the first minute she set eyes on him. With a half laugh, Shelby paced to the other end of the room. It would have done her no good. She could have fled like a crazed rabbit. Alan would have tracked her, calmly, unhurriedly. When she had collapsed, out of breath, he would just simply have been there waiting for her.

"Your tea, Miss Campbell."

Shelby turned to see McGee enter with a porcelain tea service she simply had to touch. "Oh, Meissen—red stoneware." She lifted the delicately painted, marbleized cup. "Johann Böttger, early 1700s... Wonderful." Shelby studied the cup as any art student studies the work of a master. She'd always felt museums had the right to preserve some irreplaceables behind glass while the rest should be handled, touched, and used. "He never reached his lifelong aim," she murmured, "to achieve that Oriental perfection of color decoration—but what marvelous things he produced trying."

Catching the butler's eye, Shelby realized she was being weighed as a possible gold digger. Amused, she set the cup back on the tray. "Sorry, McGee, I get carried away. I've an affection for clay."

"Clay, miss?"

She tapped a finger against the cup. "It all starts out that way. Just a lump of different sorts of dirt."

"Yes, miss." He decided it would be undignified to pursue the matter. "Perhaps you'd care to sit on the sofa."

Shelby obliged him, then watched as he carefully arranged the service on the table in front of her. "McGee...has Alan always been so quietly unbeatable?"

"Yes, miss," he answered without thinking. The phrase had been so perfectly apt.

"I was afraid so," Shelby murmured.

"I beg your pardon, miss?"

"What?" Distracted, Shelby glanced up, then shook her head. "Nothing, nothing at all. Thank you, McGee."

Shelby sipped, wondering why she had bothered to ask when she had known the answer. Alan would always win in whatever aspect of his life he concentrated on. For a moment, she stared into the pale gold tea. That was exactly what she most feared.

"What's the current price for a thought in these days of inflation?" Alan wondered aloud as he paused in the doorway. She'd looked so beautiful, he reflected. So distant. Then she glanced up with a smile that enhanced the first and erased the second.

"That was quick," Shelby complimented him and avoided the question with equal ease. "I'm afraid I admired your tea set a bit too strongly and made your butler nervous. He might be wondering if I'll slip the saucer into my bag." Setting down the cup, she rose. "Are you ready to go be charming and distinguished? You look as though you would be."

Alan lifted a brow. "I have a feeling *distinguished* comes perilously close to *sedate* in your book."

"No, you've lots of room yet," she told him as she breezed into the hall. "I'll give you a jab of you start teetering toward *sedate*."

Alan stopped her in the hall by slipping his arms around her waist. "I haven't done this in one hour and twenty-three minutes." His mouth covered hers, slowly, confidently. As her lips parted and offered he took, taking the kiss just to the border, but no further, of madness. "I love you." He caught her bottom lip between his teeth, then released her mouth only to change the angle and deepen the kiss. He felt her heartbeat sprint against his, felt that long, lazy melting of her bones he knew happened just before she went from pliant to avid. "Tonight, no matter who you dance with, think of me."

Breathless, she looked up. In his eyes, she saw that banked brooding passion she could never resist. He'd overwhelm her if she let him; absorb her. He had the power. Shelby tilted her head so her lips stayed within a whisper of his. "Tonight," she said huskily, "no matter who you dance with, you'll want me." Her arms stayed around him when she rested her head on his shoulder. "And I'll know."

Just then she caught a glimpse of them in the long beveled mirror framed on the wall. Alan, sleek and sophisticated, was as conventional in black tie as she was unorthodox in the snug velvet jacket and narrow rose-hued skirt she'd found in a shop that specialized in cast-off heirlooms. "Alan." Shelby nudged him around until he faced the mirror with her. "What do you see?"

With his arm around her waist, he studied their reflections. The top of her head came to the base of his jaw. He wondered what other redhead could have not only worn that shade of rose, but looked so stunning in it. She might have stepped out of that antique looking glass in the century in which it had been fashioned. But there was no cameo at her neck. Instead there was a thick twisted gold chain that probably came from a narrow little Georgetown shop. Her hair curled riotously, untamedly, around her pale angled face. The faint shadow of trouble in her eyes made her look more like the waif he'd first compared her to.

"I see two people in love," he said with his gaze fixed on hers in the glass. "Two very different people who look extraordinarily well together."

Shelby leaned her head on his shoulder again, unsure if she was glad or annoyed that he read her so perfectly. "He would look very good, and much more suitable, with a cool blonde in a very classic black dress."

Alan seemed to consider for a moment. "Do you know," he said mildly. "That's the first time I've heard you sound like a complete ass."

She stared back at his image, at the faintly interested, fully reasonable expression on his face. She laughed. There seemed to be nothing else for her to do. "All right, just for that, I'm going to be every bit as dignified as you are."

"God forbid," Alan muttered before he pulled her out the front door.

Elegant lighting and the sparkle of crystal. White linen tablecloths and the gleam of silver. Shelby sat at one of the more than two-dozen large round tables with Alan on one hand and the head of the Ways and Means Committee on the other. She spooned at her lobster bisque and kept up a flowing conversation.

"If you weren't so stubborn, Leo, and tried an aluminum racket, you might just see an improvement in your game."

"My game *has* improved." The balding bull-shouldered statesman shook his spoon at her. "We haven't had a match in six months. You wouldn't beat me in straight sets now."

Shelby smiled, sipping from her water glass as one course was cleared and replaced by the next. "We'll see if I can't squeeze out a couple of hours and get to the club."

"You do that. Damned if I wouldn't enjoy whipping you."

"You're going to have to watch those foot faults, Leo," she reminded him with the grin still in her eyes.

She thanked fate for seating her next to Leo. With him, she could be easy, natural. There were dozens of people in the huge high-ceilinged room she knew, and a handful she'd have been genuinely pleased to spend an hour with.

Ambition. It wafted through the room like expensive perfume. She didn't mind that, but the stiff, unbending rules and traditions that went hand in hand with it. Hand in hand with Alan, she remembered, then pushed the thought aside. She'd promised him she'd be on her best behavior. God knows she was trying.

"Then there's your weak backhand..."

"Just leave my backhand alone," he told her with a sniff. Leaning forward a bit, he frowned at Alan. "You ever played tennis with this hustler, MacGregor?"

"No, I haven't—" his eyes skimmed over to Shelby's "—yet."

"Well, I'll warn you, this little girl takes a vicious delight in winning. No respect for age either," he added as he picked up his fork.

"I'm still not going to spot you points for years, Leo," Shelby stated easily. "You have a habit of adding them indiscriminately when you're behind in sets."

A smile twitched at his mouth. "Devil," he accused. "You wait until the rematch."

With a laugh, Shelby turned back to Alan. "Do you play tennis, Senator?"

"Now and then," he said with the ghost of a smile. He didn't add he'd lettered in the sport at Harvard.

"I'd imagine chess would be your game—plotting, long-term strategy."

His smile remained enigmatic as he reached for his wine. "We'll have to have a game."

Shelby's low laugh drifted over him. "I believe we already have."

His hand brushed lightly over hers. "Want a rematch?"

Shelby gave him a look that made his blood spring hotly. "No. You might not outmaneuver me a second time."

God, but he wished the interminable meal would end. He wanted her alone—alone where he could peel off those clothes layer by layer and feel her skin warm. He could watch those laughing gray eyes cloud until he knew she thought of nothing but him. It was her scent that was hammering at his senses, not the arrangement of baby roses in the center of the table, not the aroma of food as yet another course was served. It was her voice he heard—low and just a little throaty—not the tones and textures of the voices all around him. He could talk with the congresswoman on his right, talk as if he were vitally interested in everything she told him. But he thought about holding Shelby and hearing her murmur his name when she touched him.

This sharpness of need would ease, Alan told himself. It had to. A man could go mad wanting a woman this intensely. In time it would become a more comfortable sensation—a touch in the middle of the night, a smile across the room. He glanced at her profile as she continued to tease Leo. Those sharp pixie features, that tousled flame of hair—she'd never be comfortable. The need would never ease. And she was his destiny as much as he was hers. Neither of them could stop it.

The conversations ebbed and flowed over the muted dinner music. A curtain of smoke rose up toward the ceiling from cigarettes and pipes and after-dinner cigars. Talk centered around politics, edgy at times, pragmatic at others. Whatever other topic that came up was invariably linked to the core of the world they revolved in. Alan heard Shelby give a concise and unflattering opinion of a controversial bill slated to come before Congress the following week. It infuriated the man she spoke with, though he maintained a tight-lipped control Shelby seemed implacably trying to break. Though he agreed with her stand, her tactics were... rebellious? he decided after a moment. A diplomat she would never be.

Did she know how complex she was? he wondered. Here was a woman dead set against politicians as a group, yet she could meet them on their own terms, talk to them in their own voice without revealing the slightest discomfort. If indeed she felt any, Alan added. No, if there was discomfort, it was on the opposing side. His gaze skimmed over the other people at their table as he continued his conversation with the congresswoman. Shelby didn't have their polish, their gloss. And Alan knew it was through her own choosing. More than that, she was dedicatedly opposed to possessing it. She didn't exploit the unique, she simply *was* the unique.

The sleek brunette across from him might be more beautiful, the blonde more regal—but it was Shelby you would remember when the evening was over. The representative from Ohio might have a wicked wit, the Assistant Secretary of State might be erudite—but it was Shelby you wanted to talk to. Why? The reason was there was no reason you could name. It was simply so.

He felt her shift before her lips brushed close to his ear. "Are you going to dance with me, Senator? It's the only dignified way I can get my hands on you at the moment."

Alan let the first wave of desire take him—a rush that blanked everyone else from his sight and hearing for one heady instant. Carefully he banked it before he rose and took her hand. "Strange how closely our minds work." After leading her to the dance floor he gathered her to him. "And how well," he murmured as their bodies melded together, "we fit."

Shelby tilted her head back. "We shouldn't." Her eyes promised hot, private secrets. Her lips tempted—just parted, just curved. The hand on his shoulder moved nearer to his neck so she could brush his skin with her fingertips. "We shouldn't fit. We shouldn't understand each other. I can't quite figure out why we do."

"You defy logic, Shelby. And therefore, logically, there's no reasonable answer."

She laughed, pleased with the structured workings of his mind. "Oh, Alan, you're much too sensible to be argued with."

"Which means you'll constantly do so."

"Exactly." Still smiling, she rested her head on his shoulder. "You know me too well for my own good, Alan . . . and perhaps for yours. I'm in danger of adoring you."

He remembered Myra had used that word to describe Shelby's feelings for her father. "I'll take the risk. Will you?"

With her eyes closed, she made a slight movement with her head. Neither of them knew if it was assent or denial.

As the evening wore on they danced again, each thinking of the other as they moved to the music with someone else. From time to time if they saw each other across the room a message would pass, too strong and too direct not to be observed by people whose livelihoods depended on the interpretation of a look or gesture. Undercurrents of all kinds were an intimate part of the game in Washington. Some flowed with them, others against them, but all acknowledged them.

"Well, Alan." Leo clamped a hand on Alan's shoulder as Shelby was led onto the dance floor again. "You're making some progress on your personal windmill."

Alan settled back with his wine, half-smiling. He didn't mind the allusion to Don Quixote when it came to his housing project. That sort of tag would have certain advantages in the long run. It was human nature to at least root for the underdog even if doing nothing tangible to help. "A bit. I'm beginning to get some positive feedback from Boston on the progress of the shelters there."

"It would be to your benefit if you could get and keep the ball rolling during this administration." He flipped out a lighter and flicked it at the end of a long fragrant cigar. "It should bring a lot of support your way if you decide to toss your hat in the ring."

Alan tasted the wine and watched Shelby. "It's early days yet for that, Leo."

"You know better." Leo puffed smoke toward the ceiling. "I never wanted that...particular race for myself. But you...a lot of people are willing to swing your way when the time comes, if you give the nod."

Alan turned to give his colleague a long look. "So I've been told," he said cautiously. "I appreciate it. It isn't a decision I'll make lightly, one way or the other."

"Let me give you a few pros because, bluntly, I'm not enthusiastic about what we have in the bull pen at the moment." He leaned a bit closer. "Your record's impressive—even though it leans a bit to the left for some tastes.

You had a solid run in Congress and your term as senator's running smoothly. I won't get into a point by point of your policies or your individual bills—let's stick with image." He puffed on the cigar again as he considered.

"Your youth is to your advantage. It gives us time. Your education was slick and impressive—and the fact that you did well in sports never hurts. People like to think that their leader can handle himself on any playing field. Your family background's clean and solid. The fact that your mother is a highly successful professional works strongly in your favor."

"She'll be glad to hear it," Alan said dryly.

"You're too smart to think it doesn't matter," Leo reminded him, gesturing with his cigar. "It shows that you can relate and understand professional women—a healthy chunk of the voting power. Your father has a reputation for going his own way, but going honestly. There's no hornet's nest to keep locked in the attic."

"Leo..." Alan swirled his wine before he shot Leo a direct look. "Who asked you to speak to me?"

"And you're perceptive," Leo returned without missing a beat. "Let's just say I was asked to approach you and touch on some generalities."

"All right. Generally speaking, I haven't ruled out the possibility of entering the primaries when the time comes."

"Fair enough." Leo nodded toward Shelby. "I'm personally fond of the girl. But will she be an asset to you? I never would have seen the two of you as a couple."

"Oh?" The word was mild, but Alan's eyes narrowed ever so slightly.

"Campbell's daughter—she knows the ropes, being on the campaign trail as a child." Leo pursed his lips, cautiously weighing the pros and cons. "Shelby grew up with politics, so she wouldn't have to be tutored on protocol or diplomacy. Of course, she's a bit of a maverick." He tapped his cigar thoughtfully. "More than a bit when it comes to it. She's put her considerable energy into flouting the Washington social scene for years. There are those that rather like her for it, myself for one, but she's put a few noses out of joint in her day."

Leo popped the cigar back into his mouth and chewed on it while Alan remained flatly silent. "But then, it's possible to polish off a few rough edges. She's young; the flamboyance could be toned down. Her education and family background are above reproach. There's enough glamour attached to her to attract, not enough to alienate. She runs her own business successfully and knows how to handle a crowd. An excellent choice, all in all," he decided. "If you can whip her into shape."

Alan set down his glass to prevent himself from throwing it. "Shelby isn't required to be an asset," he said in a deadly controlled voice. "She isn't required to be anything but what she chooses. Our relationship isn't grist for the political mill, Leo."

Leo frowned at the tip of his cigar. He'd touched a nerve, he realized, but was rather pleased with the manner in which Alan controlled rage. It wasn't wise to have a hothead commanding the armed forces. "I realize you feel entitled to a certain amount of privacy, Alan. But once you toss your hat in the ring, you toss your lady's in too. We're a culture of couples. One reflects the other."

Knowing it was true only infuriated him more. This was what Shelby backed away from, what she feared. How could he protect her from it and remain what he was? "Whatever I decide to do, Shelby remains free to be exactly what Shelby is." Alan rose. "That's the bottom line."

Chapter Nine

With sunshine and the best of spirits, Shelby opened the doors of Calliope Monday morning. If there had been a monsoon outside the windows, it wouldn't have jarred her mood. She had spent a long lazy Sunday with Alan, never once venturing outside her apartment. Never once wanting to.

Now Shelby sat behind the counter and decided to allow a little of the outside world into her sphere. Taking the morning paper, she opened it first, as always, to the comics. What characters would appear in Macintosh and what would they have to say for themselves? With her elbows propped, her hands supporting her chin, Shelby gave a snort of laughter. As usual Macintosh hit things on the head, but at a tilted angle that couldn't be resisted. She hoped the Vice President kept his sense of humor after he'd read his little part in this morning's column. From her experience, people in the limelight rarely objected to being caricaturized—to a point. Exposure, satirical or not, was exposure.

Shelby glanced at the signature line, the simple G.C. identifying the cartoonist. Perhaps when one hit so often and so truly at the ego, it was best to opt for anonymity. She couldn't do it, she realized. It simply wasn't in her nature to be clever anonymously.

Reaching absently for her half-cup of cooling coffee, Shelby continued down the page. Humor always eased her into the day and affirmed her view that whatever oddities there were in the world, there was a place for them. Still sipping, she glanced up as the door to the shop opened.

"Hi." With a smile for Maureen Francis, she pushed the paper aside. The brunette didn't look like a woman who'd even own a slicker, much less wear one. This morning it was silk, robin's egg blue cut into a slim spring suit. "Hey, you look great," Shelby told her, admiring the suit without imagining herself in it.

"Thanks." Maureen set a trim leather briefcase on the counter. "I came by to pick up my pottery and to thank you."

"I'll get the boxes." She slipped into the back room where she'd instructed Kyle to store them. "What do I get thanked for?" she called out.

"The contact." Unable to contain her curiosity, Maureen slipped around the counter to poke her head into Shelby's workroom. "This is wonderful," she decided, staring with layman's perplexity at the wheel before she scanned the shelves. "I'd love to watch you work sometime."

"Catch me in the right mood on a Wednesday or Saturday, and I'll give you a quick lesson if you'd like."

"Can I ask you a stupid question?"

"Sure." Shelby glanced back over her shoulder. "Everyone's entitled to three a week."

Maureen gestured to encompass the workroom and the shop. "How do you manage all this by yourself? I mean, I *know* what it's like to start your own business. It's difficult and complicated enough, but when you add this kind of creativity, the hours it takes you to produce something—then to switch gears and go into merchandising."

"That's not a stupid question," Shelby decided after a moment. "I suppose I like dipping my hands into both elements. In here, I'm normally very isolated. Out there—" she gestured toward the shop "—I'm not. And I like calling my own tune." With a grin, she began shuffling cartons. "I imagine you do, too, or you'd still be with that firm in Chicago."

"Yes, but I still have moments when I'm tempted to race back to safety." She studied Shelby's back. "I don't imagine you do."

"There's a certain amount of fun in instability, isn't there?" Shelby countered. "Especially if you believe there's bound to be a net somewhere to catch you if you slip off the edge."

With a laugh, Maureen shook her head. "That's one way of looking at it. Enjoy, and take the rest on faith."

"In a nutshell." Shelby handed Maureen the first box, then hefted the other two herself. "By the contact you mentioned, I suppose you mean Myra."

"*Mmm,* yes. I called her Saturday afternoon. All I had to do was say Shelby, and she invited me for brunch this morning."

"Myra doesn't believe in wasting time." Shelby blew her bangs out of her eyes as she set the boxes on the counter. "Will you let me know how it goes?"

"You'll be the first," Maureen promised. "You know, not everyone's so willing to hand out favors—to close friends, let alone strangers. I really appreciate it."

"You said you were good," Shelby reminded her with a grin as she started to make out a final receipt. "I thought you might be. In any event, you might not consider it so much a favor by this afternoon. Myra's a tough lady."

"So'm I." Maureen drew out her checkbook. "And an insatiably curious one. You can tell me to mind my own business," she began, glancing back up at Shelby. "But I have to ask you how things worked out with Senator

MacGregor. I'm afraid I didn't recognize him at the time. I took him for your average lovesick maniac."

Shelby considered the phrase and found it to her liking. "He's a stubborn man," she told Maureen and ripped off her copy of the receipt. "Thank God."

"Good. I like a man who thinks in rainbows. Well, I'd better get these boxes into the car if I don't want to be late."

"I'll give you a hand." Holding boxes, Shelby propped the door open so Maureen could pass.

"The car's right here." She popped open the rear door of a trim little hatchback. "I might just drop in on you on one of those Wednesdays or Saturdays."

"Fine. If I snarl, just back off until the mood passes. Good luck."

"Thanks." Maureen shut the hatch and moved around to the driver's side. "Give the Senator my regards, will you?"

Laughing, Shelby waved her away before she went back into the shop. She'd box up that green krater, she decided. This time she'd give Alan a surprise.

He was about to get one in any case—though it shouldn't have been a surprise to him.

Alan didn't often feel harassed, but this morning had been one continual stream of meetings. He didn't often feel pressured by the press, but the reporter who had been lying in wait for him outside the new Senate office building had been both tenacious and irritating. Perhaps he still carried a layer of annoyance from his conversation with Leo, or perhaps he had simply been working too hard, but by the time Alan stepped off the elevator onto his own floor of the building, his patience was strained to the breaking point.

"Senator." His assistant sprang up from her chair, looking nearly as frazzled as he felt. "The phones hardly stopped all morning." She carried a leather ledger with her and was already thumbing through it. "A Ned Brewster with the AFL-CIO; Congresswoman Platt; Shiver at the mayor's office in Boston in reference to the Back Bay Shelter; Smith, the Media Adviser; a Rita Cardova, a social worker in northeast who insists on speaking to you personally about your housing project; and—"

"Later." Alan strode through to his office and closed the door. Ten minutes—he promised himself ten minutes as he dropped his briefcase on his desk. He'd been answering a merry-go-round of demands since eight-thirty that morning. Damn if he wouldn't steal ten minutes before he hopped back on again.

It wasn't like him to need them, he thought with a sound of frustration as he frowned out the window. He could see the east side of the Capitol, the white dome symbolizing democracy, freedom of thought, justice—everything Alan had always believed in. He could see Capitol Plaza with its huge round pots filled with flowers. They'd been put in after the bombing—an aesthetic barricade. They represented what Alan knew was part of the human web. Some sought to build; some sought to destroy. Terrorism was frighteningly logical. If he, as Leo had put it, threw his hat into the ring, it was something he would have to deal with every day.

His decision couldn't be put off much longer. Oh, normally, he could bide his time, test the waters. And in essence he would do so—publicly. But privately his decision had to come soon. There'd be no asking Shelby to marry him again until he could first tell her what he was considering. He would be asking her to share more than name, home, and family if he eventually sought the presidency.

He would be asking her to elect to give a section of her life to him, to their country, to the wheels of protocol and politics. Alan no longer considered the decision to be his alone. Shelby was already his wife in all but the legal sense—he had only to convince her of that.

When the buzzer on his desk sounded, he eyed it with displeasure. He'd only had five of his ten minutes. Annoyed, he picked up the phone. "Yes?"

"I'm sorry to disturb you, Senator, but your father's on line one."

He dragged a hand through his hair as he sat. "All right, I'll take it. Arlene—*I'm* sorry, it's been a rough morning."

Her tone underwent a quick and total change. "It's okay. Your father sounds...characteristically exuberant, Senator."

"Arlene, you should have opted for the diplomatic corps." He heard her light chuckle before he switched lines. "Hello, Dad."

"Well, well, well, so you're still alive." The booming, full-bodied voice was not so subtly laced with sarcasm. "Your mother and I thought you'd met with some fatal accident."

Alan managed to keep the grin out of his voice. "I nicked myself shaving last week. How are you?"

"He asks how I am!" Daniel heaved a sigh that should have been patented for long-suffering fathers everywhere. "I wonder you even remember *who* I am. But that's all right—it doesn't matter about me. Your mother, now, she's been expecting her son to call. Her firstborn."

Alan leaned back. How often had he cursed fate for making him the eldest and giving his father that neat little phrase to needle him with? Of course, he remembered philosophically, Daniel had phrases for Rena and Caine as well—the only daughter, the youngest son. It was all relative. "Things've been a little hectic. Is Mom there?"

"Had an emergency at the hospital." Wild horses wouldn't have made Daniel admit that his wife, Anna, would have lectured him for an hour if she'd known what he was up to. Daniel considered it basic strategy not to tell her until it was done. "Since she's been moping and sighing around here," he lied without qualm, "I thought I'd bury my pride and call you myself. It's time you took a weekend and came to see your mother."

Alan lifted a wry brow, knowing his father all too well. "I'd think *she'd* be all wrapped up in her first prospective grandchild. How is Rena?"

"You can see for yourself this weekend," Daniel informed him. "I—that is, Rena and Justin have decided they want to spend a weekend with the family. Caine and Diana are coming too."

"You've been busy," Alan murmured.

"What was that? Don't mumble, boy."

"I said you'll be busy," Alan amended prudently.

"For your mother's sake, I can sacrifice my peace and quiet. She worries about all of you—you especially since you're still without wife and family. The firstborn," he added, working himself up, "and both your brother and sister settled before you. The eldest son, my own father's namesake, and too busy flitting around to do his duty to the MacGregor line."

Alan thought about his grueling morning and nearly smiled. "The MacGregor line seems to be moving along nicely. Maybe Rena'll have twins."

"Hah!" But Daniel considered the idea for a moment. He thought he recalled twins a couple of generations back on his mother's side. He made a mental note to check the family tree after he hung up. "We'll expect you Friday night. Now…'' Daniel leaned across his massive desk and puffed on one of his forbidden cigars. ''What the hell is all this I read in the papers?''

''Narrow it down for me,'' Alan suggested.

''I suppose it might have been a misprint,'' Daniel considered, frowning at the tip of his cigar before he tapped it in the ashtray he kept secreted in the bottom drawer of his desk. ''I think I know my own flesh and blood well enough.''

''Narrow it just a bit further,'' Alan requested, though he'd already gotten the drift. It was simply too good to end it too soon.

''When I read that my own son—my heir, as things are—is spending time fraternizing with a Campbell, I know it's a simple matter of a misspelling. What's the girl's name?''

Along with a surge of affection, Alan felt a tug of pure and simple mischief. ''Which girl is that?''

''Dammit, boy! The girl you're seeing who looks like a pixie. Fetching young thing from the picture I saw. Good bones; holds herself well.''

''Shelby,'' Alan said, then waited a beat. ''Shelby Campbell.''

Dead silence. Leaning back in his chair, Alan wondered how long it would be before his father remembered to take a breath. It was a pity, he mused, a real pity that he couldn't see the old pirate's face.

''*Campbell!*'' The word erupted. ''A thieving, murdering Campbell!''

''Yes, she's fond of MacGregors as well.''

''No son of mine gives the time of day to one of the clan Campbell!'' Daniel bellowed. ''I'll take a strap to you, Alan Duncan MacGregor!'' The threat was as empty now as it had been when Alan had been eight, but delivered in the same full-pitched roar. "I'll wear the hide off you."

"You'll have the chance to try this weekend when you meet Shelby."

"A Campbell in *my* house! Hah!"

"A Campbell in your house," Alan repeated mildly. "And a Campbell in your family before the end of the year if I have my way."

"You—" Emotions warred in him. A Campbell versus his firmest aspiration: to see each of his children married and settled, and himself laden with grandchildren. "You're thinking of marriage to a Campbell?"

"I've already asked her. She won't have me...yet," he added.

"Won't have you!" Paternal pride dominated all else. "What kind of a nitwit is she? Typical Campbell," he muttered. "Mindless pagans." Daniel suspected they'd had some sorcerers sprinkled among them. "Probably bewitched the boy," he mumbled, scowling into space. "Always had good sense before this. Aye, you bring your Campbell to me," he ordered roundly. "I'll get to the bottom of it."

Alan smothered a laugh, forgetting the poor mood that had plagued him only minutes earlier. "I'll ask her."

"*Ask?* Hah! You bring the girl, that daughter of a Campbell, here."

Picturing Shelby, Alan decided he wouldn't miss the meeting for two-thirds of the popular vote. "I'll see you Friday, Dad. Give Mom my love."

"Friday," Daniel murmured, puffing avidly on his cigar. "Aye, aye, Friday."

As he hung up Alan could all but see his father rubbing his huge hands together in anticipation. It should be an interesting weekend.

* * *

When he pulled up in the alleyway beside Shelby's town house, Alan forgot his fatigue. The ten-hour day was behind him, with all its reams of paperwork, facts, and figures.

But when Shelby opened the door to him, she saw the weariness and the dregs of annoyance still in his eyes. "Bad day for democracy?" With a smile, she took his face in her hands and kissed him lightly.

"Long," he corrected and pulled her closer for a more satisfactory embrace. And he knew he could face a hundred more like it if he just had her when it was over. "Sorry I'm late."

"You're not. You're here. Want a drink?"

"I wouldn't turn one down."

"Come on, I'll pretend I'm domestic for a few minutes." Shelby led him in to the couch. After nudging him down, she loosened his tie herself, drew it off, then undid the top two buttons of his shirt. Alan watched with a half-grin as she pulled off his shoes. "I could get used to this."

"Well, don't," she advised on her way to the bar. "You never know when you'll come in and find me collapsed on the couch and refusing to budge."

"Then I'll pamper you," he offered as she handed him a Scotch. Shelby sat down to curl beside him. "I needed this."

"The drink?"

"You." When she tilted back her head, he gave her a long lingering kiss. "Just you."

"You want to tell me about all the nasty officials or lobbyists or whatever that messed up your day."

He laughed and let the Scotch linger on his tongue. "I had a rather lengthy go-round with Congresswoman Platt."

"Martha Platt." Shelby let out a knowing sigh. "She was a hard-line, opinionated, penny-pinching bureaucrat when I was a girl."

The description suited to a tee. "Still is."

"My father always said she'd have made an excellent CPA. She thinks in fiscal dollars and cents."

Laughing, he set down his glass. Who needed Scotch when he had Shelby? "What about you? How are things in the business world?"

"Slow this morning, hectic this afternoon. I had a flood of college students. It seems pottery is in. Speaking of which, I have something for you." She sprang up and dashed away while Alan stretched out his legs and realized he wasn't tired at all—just more relaxed than he would have believed possible even twenty minutes before.

"A present," Shelby told him as she set a box in his lap. "It might not be as romantic as your style, but it is unique." She dropped back down beside him as Alan flipped the lid from the box.

In silence, he lifted out the krater, cupping the bowl in both hands. Somehow she'd pictured him holding it that way, as one of the Roman leaders might have done. Seeing it in his hands gave her pleasure.

Alan studied it without speaking. It was smooth and deeply green with faint hints of something lighter just beneath the surface. The lines were clean and simple, exquisite in the very lack of decoration. He could think of nothing he'd been given that had seemed more important.

"Shelby, it's beautiful. Really, really beautiful." Shifting it to one hand, he took hers with the other. "It's fascinated me, right from the start, that such small hands hold such large talent." He kissed her fingers before his eyes lifted to hers. "Thank you. You were making this the day I came into your workroom."

"You don't miss much, do you?" Pleased, she ran a finger down the side of the bowl. "I was making it . . . and thinking of you. It seemed only right that you should have it when it was finished. Then when I saw your house, I knew it was right for you."

"It's right for me," he agreed before he settled the krater back in its box. Setting it carefully on the floor, he drew her close again. "So are you."

She rested her head on his shoulder. It seemed true when he said it. "Let's send out for Chinese."

"*Hmm*. I thought you wanted to see that movie down the street."

"That was this morning. Tonight I'd rather eat sweet and sour pork and neck with you on the couch. In fact," she considered as she began to nibble on his neck, "I could probably make do with a few stale crackers and some cheese."

Alan turned so his lips could toy with hers. "How about we neck first and eat later?"

"You have such a well-ordered mind," Shelby commented as she eased back against the jumble of pillows, drawing him with her. "I just love the way it works. Kiss me, Alan, the way you did when we first sat here. It drove me mad."

Her eyes were half-closed, her lips just parted. Alan tangled his fingers in the hair that tumbled wildly over the bold odd-shaped pillows. He didn't feel the patience now he had forced himself to feel that first time. With Shelby, imagining what it would be like wasn't nearly as arousing as knowing what it was like. She was more titillating than the most pagan fantasy, more desirable than any fevered dream. And she was here, for him.

Alan tasted her lips slowly, as she had wanted him to. The need to devour could be controlled when he knew there would be a time for it. She sighed, then trembled. The combination nearly pushed him over the edge before he'd realized he'd been that close to it. He hadn't even touched her but for that light, teasing play of mouth on mouth.

He hadn't known torture could be so exquisite. But he knew the sweet allure of agony now, with his mouth fastened on Shelby's, with her fingers opening his shirt to explore him.

She loved the feel of him. Each time she could touch him freely, Shelby knew she'd never tire of doing so. It always brought such pure pleasure, such sharp greed. Always when she saw something she admired, she wanted to test the feel of it, the weight, the texture. It was no different with Alan. Yet each time she did, it might have been the first.

The scent of his soap—no, her soap, she remembered—lingered on him, but with the faint musky fragrance the day had worked on him. His heart beat quickly, though his mouth still made love to hers with slow, enervating thoroughness. Her fingers slid up to his shoulders to push the shirt away, to explore with more liberty. His kiss lost its patience with an abruptness that left her breathless.

Now she was spinning through the storm he could conjure like a magician. Boiling black clouds, bold lightning. She could have sworn she heard thunder, but it was only the thud of her own pulse. His hands were quick, undressing her in something like a rage, then molding her with hard, sure strokes that had her passing from one convulsive shudder to another. She crested rapidly, mindlessly, without the control to do any more than spin with the tempest.

He heard her call to him, but he was too tangled in his own web to answer. The lazy, satiating love of the day before hadn't done this to him. There was something wild in him, something fierce that had never been given full freedom. It came now, like the panther would come if it finally tore free of its cage. He was ravaging her, and even knowing it, couldn't stop. Her body was eager and trembling beneath his. Everywhere his mouth touched he tasted passion and promise.

She arched, moaning. With his tongue, he drove her ruthlessly to another peak. Her body was on fire, her mind wiped clean of thought, to be ruled only by sensations. She didn't know what he asked her, though she heard the urgent huskiness of his voice. She didn't know what she answered, only that nothing he could have demanded would have been too much. Dimly through the curtain of passion, she saw his face above hers. His eyes weren't brooding, that was all that was clear. They were dark, almost savage.

"I can't live without you," he said in a whisper that seemed to echo endlessly in her head. "I won't."

Then his mouth crushed down on hers, and everything was lost in the delirium.

"Sure you don't want any more?"

Two hours later Shelby sat cross-legged on the bed in a skimpy Japanese-print silk robe that left her legs bare. She stuck her fork into a little white cardboard carton and scooped out some cooling sweet and sour pork. Behind her the television played on low volume with no picture at all. Alan stayed comfortably stretched out, his head propped on her pillows.

"No." He watched her dig for more. "Shelby, why don't you get that set fixed?"

"*Mmm,* sooner or later," she said vaguely before she set the carton aside. Pushing a hand against her stomach she sighed lustily. "I'm stuffed." With a considering smile on her face, she let her gaze wander down from his face over his leanly muscled body. "I wonder how many people in the Washington metropolitan area know just how terrific Senator MacGregor looks in his underwear."

"A select few."

"You must have thought about image projection, Senator." She ran a fingertip down the top of his foot. "You should consider doing some of those ads, you know, like the ball players...I never meet with foreign dignitaries without my B.V.D.'s."

"One can only be grateful you're not the Media Adviser."

"Stuffy, that's the whole problem." She dropped, full-length, on top of him. "Just think of the possibilities."

Alan slipped a hand under her robe. "I am."

"Discreetly placed ads in national magazines, thirty-minute spots in prime time." Shelby propped her elbows on his shoulders. "I'd definitely get my set fixed."

"Think of the trend it might start. Federal official everywhere stripped down to their respective shorts.

Shelby's brows drew together as she pictured it. "Good God, it could precipitate a national calamity."

"Worldwide," Alan corrected. "Once the ball got rolling, there'd be no stopping it."

"All right, you've convinced me." She gave him a smacking kiss. "It's your patriotic duty to keep your clothes on. Except in here," she added with a gleam in her eye as she toyed with his waistband.

Laughing, he drew her mouth back to his. "Shelby..." Her tongue skimmed over his while he cupped the back of her neck more firmly. "Shelby," he repeated a moment later, "there was something I wanted to talk to you about earlier, and I'm in danger of becoming as distracted now as I was then.''

"Promise?" She moved her lips to his throat.

"I have a command performance this weekend."

"Oh?" She switched to his ear.

In self-defense, Alan rolled over and pinned her beneath him. "I got a call from my father this afternoon."

"Ah." Humor danced in her eyes. "The laird."

"The title would appeal to him." Alan grasped her wrists to prevent her from clouding his mind as she seemed bent on doing. "It seems he's planned one of his famous family weekends. Come with me."

One brow lifted. "To the MacGregor fortress in Hyannis Port? Unarmed?"

"We'll hoist the white flag."

She wanted to go. She wanted to say no. A visit to his family home came perilously close to that final commitment she was so carefully sidestepping. Questions, speculation—there'd be no avoiding them. Alan heard her thought as clearly as if it had been spoken. Pushing back frustration, he changed tactics.

"I have orders to bring that girl—" he watched her eyes narrow "—that daughter of the thieving, murdering Campbells, with me."

"Oh, is that so?"

"Just so," Alan returned mildly.

Shelby lifted her chin. "When do we leave?"

Chapter Ten

Shelby's first thought when she saw the house on the cliff was that she couldn't have done better herself. It was glorious. Rough, unpampered, it sat high with towers rising and turrets jutting. It was made of stone and hinted of the sea—gloomy and mysterious in the lowering light. A fortress, a castle, an anachronism—she wouldn't label it, only appreciate.

When she turned to Alan, Shelby saw that his brow was lifted as he waited for her verdict. There was that touch of humor in his eyes she'd learned to detect, and the irony that went with it. On a laugh, she leaned on the dash again to look her fill.

"You knew I'd love it."

Because he couldn't resist, Alan reached forward just to touch his fingertips to her hair. "I thought it might... appeal to you."

Shelby chuckled at the dry tone and continued to look at the house while Alan drove the rented car up the sloping road. "If I'd grown up here, I'd have had headless ghosts for playmates and kept my room in a tower."

Alan maneuvered around one of the winding curves that only added to the atmosphere. The sea was close enough so its scent and sound drifted in the open windows. "There aren't any ghosts, though my father periodically threatened to import a few bloodthirsty ones from Scotland."

With his lips just curved, he sent Shelby a quick sidelong look. "He keeps his office in a tower room."

She turned, lifted a brow, then leaned on the dash again. "Hmm." Brows still arched, she studied the slit windows of the tower. Daniel MacGregor. Yes, she was looking forward to meeting him, she decided. Even if it was on his home turf. But before she did, Shelby was going to enjoy the view.

The flowers were a nice touch, she reflected—rivers of them flowing out from the base of the house in a wild concoction of spring fancy. Did The MacGregor have the last say on the landscaping as well, Shelby wondered, or was this his wife's province? Perhaps the thoracic surgeon relaxed by planting petunias. Shelby considered and decided it made sense. Clever hands and a clever mind would need just that sort of creative outlet.

If the house had been Daniel's design and the gardens Anna's, Shelby concluded they must suit each other very well. Both aspects were unique, strong, and unapologetic. Meeting them, she mused, might prove very interesting.

No sooner had Alan stopped the car than Shelby was climbing out to dash to the edge of a flower bed where she could stand and take in the whole structure at once. She was laughing again, her head thrown back, the unmanageable curls tossing in the wind. In the gloaming, she thought the house would be at its best.

Alan leaned against the hood of the car and watched her. With Shelby, sometimes watching was enough.

He liked the look of her against the backdrop of wildly colored flowers and the dull stone of the house, with her hands in the pockets of loosely fitting trousers, the thin material of her blouse rippling in the wind. The tiny tulips decorating the neckline had been painstakingly stitched more than fifty years before. She wore a slim digital watch on her wrist.

"I'd definitely have had ghosts," she decided, then held out her hand to him. "Fierce, clanking ghosts, none of those moony, ethereal types." Her fingers linked with Alan's, and for a moment, they looked up at the house together. "Kiss me, MacGregor," she demanded as she tossed windblown hair out of her eyes. "Hard. I've never seen a more perfect spot for it."

Even as she spoke her body was pressing against his, her free hand running firmly up his back to bring him close. When their mouths met, she thought she could smell a storm at sea—no matter that the skies were clear. She could touch him and feel the shivering jolt of lightning. If he whispered her name as their lips moved together, she could hear thunder.

Then they were straining against each other, lost, oblivious of the world that had simply come to a halt around them. There might have been seabirds coming to nest as night approached; the moon might have started its slow, slow rise even as the sun descended. It didn't matter. Their world had its center in each other.

Her hands brushed over his cheeks and remained lightly on his skin as they drew apart. Regret washed over her for what she couldn't yet give him, for what she might never be able to give him. A commitment that could transcend all fear, all doubt, and a promise she had made to herself.

"I love you, Alan," she murmured. "Believe it."

In her eyes, he could see the clouds of passion, and the struggle. Yes, she loved him, but... Not yet, Alan ordered himself. He could wait just a bit longer before he pressed her for more. "I believe it," he said as he took her wrists. Gently he kissed both her hands before slipping an arm around her waist. "Come inside."

Shelby tilted her head just enough to rest it briefly on his shoulder as they walked to the door. "I'm relying on your word that I'll walk out again in one piece at the end of the weekend."

He only grinned. "I told you my stand on playing the mediator."

"Thanks a lot." She glanced up at the door, noting the heavy brass crest that served as a door knocker. The MacGregor lion stared coolly at her with its Gaelic motto over its crowned head. "Your father isn't one to hide his light under a bushel, is he?"

"Let's just say he has a strong sense of family pride." Alan lifted the knocker, then let it fall heavily against the thick door. Shelby imagined the sound would vibrate into every nook and cranny in the house. "The Clan MacGregor," Alan began in a low rolling burr, "is one of the few permitted to use the crown in their crest. Good blood. Strong stock."

"Hah!" Shelby's disdainful look turned to one of mild curiosity as Alan burst out with a roar of laughter. "Something funny?"

Before he could answer, the door swung open. Shelby saw a tall man, blond with arresting blue eyes that hinted toward violet. He had a lean face that spoke of intelligence and cunning. Leaning against the door, he gave Alan a quick grin. "You can laugh," he said. "Dad's been ranting and muttering for an hour. Something about—" his gaze shifted and lingered on Shelby "—traitors and infidels. Hello, you must be the infidel."

The friendly irony in his voice had Shelby's lips curving. "I must be."

"Shelby Campbell, my brother, Caine."

"The first Campbell ever to step into the MacGregor keep. Enter at your own risk." Caine offered his hand as

Shelby crossed the threshold. His first thought was that she had the face of a mermaid—not quite beautiful, but alluring and not easily forgotten.

Shelby glanced around the wide hall, approving the faded tapestries and heavy old furniture. She caught the scent of spring flowers, a wisp of dust and old polish. No, she couldn't have done it better herself. "Well, the roof didn't cave in," she commented as she studied a crested shield on the wall. "So far so good."

"Alan!" Serena came down the stairs quickly despite the encumbrance of pregnancy. Shelby saw an elegant violet-eyed woman with hair somehow both delicate and richly blonde. She saw, too, pleasure, love, humor, before Serena threw her arms around Alan's neck. "I've missed you."

"You look beautiful, Rena." Gently he laid a hand on the mound of her belly. His sister, he thought as wonder and pride mixed together. His baby sister. "I can't get used to it," he murmured.

Serena put her hand on his. "You don't have a great deal more time to get used to it." She felt the baby move under their joined hands and grinned as Alan's gaze dropped to them. "He or she is impatient to begin." Tilting her head, she studied Alan's face. "Dad's suddenly gotten it into his head there might be two...I wonder who might have planted that seed?"

His eyes smiled as he lifted them to his sister's. "It was purely a defensive maneuver."

"*Mmm-hmm.*" Turning, she held out both hands. "You must be Shelby. I'm glad you could come."

Shelby felt the warmth, more carefree than Alan's, the welcome, less curious than Caine's. "So am I. I've been wanting to meet the woman who broke Alan's nose."

With a muffled chuckle, Serena jerked her head toward Caine. "It was supposed to be his." She narrowed her eyes a moment as Caine dipped his hands into his pockets and grinned. "It *should* have been his. Come on in and meet the rest of the family," she continued as she tucked her arm through Shelby's. "God, I hope Alan prepared you."

"In his own way."

"If you start to feel overwhelmed, just shoot me a look. These days all I have to do is sigh to distract Dad's attention for an hour and a half."

Alan looked after the two women as they walked down the hall. "Looks like Rena's taking it from here," he murmured.

Caine gave a crooked grin as he draped an arm over his brother's shoulder. "The truth is we've all been dying to see your Campbell since Dad made his, uh, announcement." He didn't ask Alan if it was serious—he didn't have to. He cast another speculative look at Shelby as they, too, started down the hall. "I hope you told her that Dad's all bark and no bite."

"Now, why would I do that?"

Shelby had a moment to take in the scene in the drawing room as she paused in the doorway. There was a dark man, smoking calmly, in an old bulky chair. Shelby had the impression that while he hardly seemed to move at all, he could move quickly when necessary. On the arm of his chair, sat a woman with the same coloring. Her hands were folded neatly on the lap of her vivid green skirt. A striking couple, Shelby mused. Then, it seemed the Mac-Gregors were a striking crowd.

Across from them was a woman working serenely with embroidery hoop and needle. Shelby could see not only where Alan got his features but that appealing, serious smile. In the center of the group, was a wide high-back chair, ornately carved. It suited the man who sat in it.

Shelby noted that Daniel MacGregor was massive. A dramatic-looking man with flaming red hair, shoulders like a tank and a lined, florid face. She saw, with a twinge of amusement, that he wore the MacGregor plaid sashed across his suit jacket. He was, indisputably, holding court.

"Rena should be getting more rest," he stated, shoving a wide blunt-edged finger at the man in the chair. "A woman in her condition's got no business being in a casino till all hours."

Justin blew out a long lazy stream of smoke. "The casino *is* Serena's business."

"When a woman's with child..." Daniel paused long enough to shoot Diana an inquiring look. Shelby watched the dark woman struggle with a grin before she shook her head. Daniel sighed, then turned back to Justin. "When a woman's with child—"

"She can function like any other healthy woman," Serena finished for him.

Before Daniel could bluster out with whatever retort he had in mind, he spotted Shelby. His broad shoulders lifted, his wide chin tilted to a stubborn angle. "Well," he said briefly and left it at that.

"Shelby Campbell," Serena began smoothly as she swept into the room with Shelby at her side. "The rest of our family. My husband, Justin Blade." Shelby found herself fixed with a pair of very calm, very shrewd green eyes. He took his time about smiling, but when he did, it was worth it. "My sister-in-law, Diana."

"You're related." Shelby cut into the introductions as she studied both Justin and Diana. "Brother and sister?"

Diana nodded, liking the candor in Shelby's eyes. "That's right."

"What tribe?" she asked.

Justin smiled again as he blew out another stream of smoke. "Comanche."

"Good stock," Daniel stated with a thump of his hand on the arm of his chair. Shelby sent him a silent look.

"My mother," Serena continued, swallowing a chuckle.

"We're so pleased you could come, Shelby." Anna's voice was quiet, soothing. Her hand, when it took Shelby's was firm and strong.

"Thank you. I was admiring your garden, Dr. MacGregor. It's spectacular."

Anna smiled, giving Shelby's hand a quick squeeze. "Thank you. It's one of my vanities." When Daniel cleared his throat, loudly, a flicker of amusement crossed Anna's face. "Did you have a good flight?" she asked easily.

"Yes." With her back to Daniel, Shelby grinned. "Very smooth."

"Let me get a look at the girl!" Daniel demanded with another thump on the arm of his chair.

Shelby heard Serena muffle another chuckle. Slowly she turned to face Daniel. Her chin was lifted at the same arrogant angle as his own. "Shelby Campbell," Alan said, enjoying the moment, "my father, Daniel MacGregor."

"Campbell," Daniel repeated, tapping both wide hands on the arms of his chair.

Shelby moved to him but didn't offer her hand. "Aye," she said because her blood seemed to demand it. "Campbell."

Daniel turned the corners of his mouth down and drew his brows together in what he considered his most formidable look. Shelby didn't blink. "My kin would sooner have a badger in their house than a Campbell."

Alan saw his mother open her mouth and shook his head to silence her. He not only knew Shelby could hold her own but wanted to see her do it.

"Most MacGregors were comfortable enough with badgers in the parlor."

"Barbarians!" Daniel sucked in his breath. "The Campbells were barbarians, each and every one of them."

Shelby tilted her head as if to study him from a new angle. "The MacGregors have a reputation for being sore losers."

Instantly Daniel's face went nearly as red as his hair. "Losers? Hah! There's never been a Campbell born who could stand up to a MacGregor in a fair fight. Backstabbers."

"We'll have Rob Roy's biography again in a minute," Shelby heard Caine mutter. "You don't have a drink, Dad," he said, hoping to distract him. "Shelby?"

"Yes." She shifted her gaze to him, noting he was doing his best to maintain sobriety. "Scotch," she told him, with a quick irrepressible wink. "Straight up. If the MacGregors had been wiser," she continued without missing a beat, "perhaps they wouldn't have lost their land and their kilts and the name. Kings," she want on mildly as Daniel began to huff and puff, "have a habit of getting testy when someone's trying to overthrow them."

"*Kings!*" Daniel exploded. "An English king, by God! No true Scotsman needed an English king to tell him how to live on his land."

Shelby's lips curved as Caine handed her a glass. "That's a truth I can drink to."

"Hah!" Daniel lifted his glass and drained it in one swallow before he thumped it onto the table at his side. Cocking a brow, Shelby eyed the Scotch in her glass, then proceeded to follow Daniel's example.

For a moment, he frowned at the empty glass beside his. Slowly, with the room deadly silent, he shifted his gaze back to Shelby. His eyes were fierce, hers insolent. Heaving himself out of his chair, he towered over her, a great bear of a man with fiery hair. She put both hands on her hips, a willow-slim woman with curls equally dramatic. Alan wished fleetingly he could paint.

Daniel's laugh, when he threw back his head and let it loose, was rich and loud and long. "Aye, by God, here's a lass!"

Shelby found herself swept off her feet in a crushing hug that held welcome.

It didn't take long for Shelby to sketch a mental outline of the MacGregor family. Daniel was bold, dramatic, and demanding—and an absolute marshmallow when it came to his children. Anna had eyes and a temperament like her eldest son. She could, Shelby concluded, quietly dominate anyone, including her husband. Watching her throughout the evening, Shelby realized she would have to stay on her toes with Alan. He had his mother's patience and her insight. A formidable combination.

She liked Alan's family—the similarities and the contrasts. Individually she would have found them interesting. As a group, she found them fascinating. The house itself was something Shelby could never have resisted. Vaulted ceilings, gargoyles, odd suits of armor, and endless passages. They ate dinner in a dining hall as big as the average house. Spears were crossed over an enormous fireplace now filled with greenery rather than blazing logs. Windows were high and leaded, but light came from an enormous Waterford chandelier. Wealth, its eccentricities and ostentations, suited Daniel MacGregor.

Shelby sat on Daniel's left and ran her finger around the rim of her dinner plate. "This is a beautiful setting," she commented. "Wedgwood's jasperware, late eighteenth century. The yellow's very rare."

"My grandmother's," Anna told her. "Her one and only prize. I'm afraid I didn't realize the color was rare."

"Blues, lavenders, greens, and blacks are produced more commonly by oxide staining. I've never seen this tone outside of a museum."

"Never understood all the fuss over a plate," Daniel put in.

"Because you're more interested in what goes on it," Serena commented.

"Shelby's a potter," Alan said mildly before his father could retort.

"A potter?" Daniel's brows drew together as he studied her. "You make pots?"

"Among other things," Shelby said dryly.

"Our mother made pottery," Diana murmured. "I remember her working at a little manual wheel when I was a girl. It's fascinating to see what can be made out of a little ball of clay. Do you remember, Justin?"

"Yes. She sometimes sold her pieces to the little store in town. Do you sell your work?" he asked Shelby. "Or is it a hobby?"

"I have a shop in Georgetown." She sensed a strong bond between brother and sister.

"A shopkeeper." Daniel nodded in approval. Commerce was something he appreciated. "You sell your own wares, then. Are you clever at it?"

Shelby lifted her wine. "I like to think so." Tossing her bangs out of her eyes, she turned to Alan. "Would you say I was clever at it, Senator?"

"Amazingly so," he returned. "For someone without any sense of organization, you manage to work at your craft, run a shop, and live precisely as you choose."

"I like odd compliments," Shelby decided after a moment. "Alan's accustomed to a more structured routine. He'd never run out of gas on the freeway."

"I like odd insults," Alan murmured into his wine.

"Makes a good balance." Daniel gestured at both of them with his fork. "Know your own mind, don't you, girl?"

"As much as anyone."

"You'll make a good First Lady, Shelby Campbell."

Shelby's fingers tightened on her wineglass, an involuntary gesture noticed only by Alan and his mother. "Perhaps," she returned calmly, "if it were one of my ambitions."

"Ambition or not, it's fate when you're paired with this one." Daniel stabbed his fork toward Alan.

"You're a little premature." Alan cut cleanly through his meat, swearing fluidly in his mind only. "I haven't decided to run for president, and Shelby hasn't agreed to marry me."

"Haven't decided? Hah!" Daniel swilled down wine. "Hasn't agreed?" He set down the glass with a bang. "The girl doesn't look like a fool to me, Campbell or no," he continued. "She's good Scottish stock, no matter what her clan. This one'll breed true MacGregors."

"He'd still like me to change my name," Justin commented, deliberately trying to shift the attention onto himself.

"It's been done to ensure the line before," Daniel told him. "but Rena's babe'll be as much MacGregor as not. As will Caine's when he's a mind to remember his duty and start making one." He sent his younger son a lowered-brow look that was met with an insolent grin. "But Alan's the firstborn, duty-bound to marry and produce and sire..."

Alan turned, intending on putting an end to the topic, when he caught Shelby's grin. She'd folded her arms on the table, forgetting her dinner in the pure enjoyment of watching Daniel MacGregor on a roll. "Having fun?" Alan muttered near her ear.

"Wouldn't miss it. Is he always like this?"

Alan glanced over, watching his father gesture with his lecture. "Yes."

Shelby sighed. "I think I'm in love. Daniel..." She interrupted his flow of words by tugging sharply on his sleeve. "No offense to Alan, or to your wife, but I think if I were going to marry a MacGregor, he'd have to be you."

Still caught up in his own diatribe, Daniel stared at her. Abruptly his features shifted and his laugh rang out. "You're a pistol, you are, Shelby Campbell. Here..." He lifted a bottle of wine. "Your glass is empty."

"That was well-done," Alan told her later as he gave Shelby a limited tour of the house.

"Was it?" Laughing, she linked her hand with his. "He's a difficult man to resist." She rose on her toes to nibble his earlobe. "So's his firstborn."

"That term's to be used reverently," Alan warned her. "Personally I've always found it a pain in the—"

"Oh, this is fabulous!" Shelby lifted a glassy porcelain vase from a high table. "French Chantilly. Alan, I swear this house is better than a sunken galleon. I'd never get tired of wandering from one corridor to another." After setting the vase down, she turned to grin at him. "Did you ever climb into one of those suits of armor?"

"Caine did once—it took me over an hour to pry him out."

Shelby gave a murmur of sympathy as she framed his face with her hands. "You were such a good boy." Her laugh was muffled against his lips in a sudden searing kiss. All heat, all fire, without a moment's warning.

"He climbed in," Alan continued as he tugged her hair back to deepen the kiss, "because I suggested it might be an interesting experience."

Breathless, Shelby stared up at him. When would she be prepared for those sudden dangerous turns of his nature? "An instigator," she managed.

"An objective leader," he corrected before he released her. "And I did manage to get him out...after he'd scared the wits out of Rena."

For a moment she leaned against the wall watching him, while the throbbing in her body slowly, very slowly, lessened. "I don't believe you were nearly as well-mannered as you once told me. You probably deserved that broken nose."

"Caine deserved it more."

Shelby laughed again as they moved down another corridor. "I like your family."

"So do I."

"And you enjoyed watching me go nose-to-nose with your father."

"I've always been fond of drawing-room comedies."

"Drawing room? It's more like a throne room." She leaned her head against his shoulder. "It's wonderful. Alan...where did your father get the idea we were going to be married?"

He flicked on a switch that brought a rather gloomy light into the hallway. "I told him I'd asked you," he said easily. "My father has a difficult time understanding that anyone could refuse his firstborn.'' Alan turned, effectively trapping Shelby between the wall and himself.

The dim light deepened the hollows in his face, casting his eyes into shadow. She could feel the strength from him though their bodies were barely touching. He could be fierce, she knew, just as easily as he could be gentle. ''Alan...''

''How long are you going to ask me to wait?'' He hadn't intended to press; had promised himself he wouldn't. But seeing her in his childhood home, with his family, with his memories, had only intensified his need for her. For all of her. ''I love you, Shelby.''

''I know.'' Her arms went around him, her cheek pressed against his. ''I love you. Give me a little more time, Alan, just a little more time. It's too much to ask, I know.'' She held on tightly a moment before she drew away far enough to see his face. ''You're more fair than I, kinder, more patient. I have to take advantage of that.''

He didn't feel fair or kind or patient. He wanted to back her into a corner and demand, insist—beg. There was too much MacGregor in him to allow for the last, and the look in her eyes wouldn't permit him to resort to the first two. ''All right. But, Shelby, there are things we have to talk about when we're back in Washington. Once I make my decision, I'll have to ask you to make yours.''

She moistened her lips, afraid she knew what his decision related to. Not now, she told herself. She wouldn't think about it now. In Washington, she would make herself deal with it, but here, now, she wanted Alan to herself with no cloud of politics, no hints of the future. ''We'll talk in Washington,'' she agreed. ''And I promise you an answer.''

Nodding, Alan circled her throat with his hand. ''Make it the one I want,'' he murmured, then kissed her with no patience at all. "It's late," he added, knowing she was both surprised and vulnerable as he continued to take greedy possession of her mouth. "I imagine everyone's gone to bed."

"We should go too."

He laughed, capturing her earlobe between his teeth. "How about a midnight swim?"

"Swim?" On a sigh, Shelby closed her eyes and let the sensations take her. "I didn't bring a suit."

"Good." Alan led her down the hall to two large double doors. After pulling them open, he nudged Shelby inside, then closed and locked the doors behind them.

"Well." With her hands on her hips, she surveyed the room.

It was large, as was typical of everything in the house. One wall was entirely glassed with huge lush plants hung at staggered levels. Shelby could see the moonlight ripple through. The floor was made of tiny mosaic tiles in an intricate pattern of blues and greens. Centered in the room was an enormous blue-tinted pool.

"Daniel MacGregor doesn't piddle around, does he?" Her voice echoed hollowly off the water from the high ceiling. With a grin, Shelby turned back to Alan. "I bet you swam every day of your life. The first time I saw you I had this flash of a channel swimmer, marathon. It's the way you're built." She gave his shoulder a quick squeeze. "Maybe I wasn't so far off."

Alan only smiled and drew her away from the pool. "We'll have a sauna first."

"Oh, will we?"

"Yeah." He hooked a hand in the waistband of her trousers and drew her closer. "Open the pores a bit." In a quick move, he unhooked them, then drew them over her hips.

"Since you insist." Shelby began undoing his tie. "Have you noticed, Senator, that most of the time you wear a great many more clothes than I?"

"As a matter of fact…" He slipped his hands under her blouse and found her. "I have."

Her fingers fumbled on his buttons. "Unless you want to take your sauna fully dressed, you'll have to stop." Letting out a long breath, Shelby tugged off his shirt. "We'll need towels," she added, then ran her hands in one long stroke down his chest to his belt.

Slowly Alan slid the blouse from her shoulders, allowing himself a lengthy look at her before he reached to the shelf behind him for towels. She was pale, slender—alluring and challenging—and his. Keeping her eyes on his, Shelby draped the towel saronglike around her.

Dry heat rushed over her when Alan opened the door to the small room. Shelby stood still a moment, absorbing it, before she moved to a bench. "I haven't done this in months," she murmured, then shut her eyes and leaned back. "It's wonderful."

"I'm told my father cemented a number of profitable deals in this room." Alan eased down beside her.

Shelby opened her eyes to slits. "I imagine he did. By the time he was through, he could've reduced most normally built men to puddles." Idly she trailed a fingertip down Alan's thigh. "Do you ever use saunas for vital government intrigue, Senator?"

"I'm inclined to think of other things in small hot rooms." Bending, he brushed his lips over her bare shoulder—the touch of a tongue, the quick pressure of teeth. "Vital, certainly, but more personal."

"*Mmm.*" Shelby tilted her head as he trailed his lips closer to her throat. "How personal?"

"Highly confidential." Alan drew her into his lap and began those slow nibbling kisses that always drugged her. Her mouth moved against his with lazy heat-soaked passion. "Your body fascinates me, Shelby. Slender, smooth, agile." His lips trailed down further, to linger just above the loose knot in the towel. "And your mind—that's agile, too, and as clever as your hands. I've never been clear which attracted me first. Perhaps it was both at once."

She was content to lie back and let him make love to her with words and with the gentle brush of lips. Her muscles were lax from the heat, her skin soft and damp. When his lips came back to hers, she found she hardly had the strength to lift her arm around his neck and bring him closer. But her mouth could move, to slant against his, to open, to invite, to entice. She concentrated all her power there as her body seemed to melt from the heat and the longing.

While he kissed her, slowly, deeply, his fingertip nudged the knot of the towel until it loosened, leaving her vulnerable to him.

He felt her moan once against his mouth, tasted the trembling breath as it merged with his own. Her scent, always exciting, seemed to fill the tiny room until there was nothing else. So he touched her, first with lazy possession, seeing each sensitive curve in his mind's eye as his fingertips glided.

With his arm hooked around her back, he drew her closer. Skin, slick from the heat, seemed to fuse together. Their lips, still hungry, drew more and more in a kiss that hinted of forever. There was response wherever he touched, response that became more frantic as his hands sought less patiently. When she began to shudder, he felt a fresh thrill rip through him. Now, it demanded. Take her now, here and now. On an unsteady breath, he forced the need aside and pleasured himself by shattering her sanity.

He found her hot and moist. When she arched against his hand, he felt her passion build then explode. Mindlessly she moaned his name, and only his name. It was all he wanted to hear. Then she was pliant again, limp and soft. He could have held her just so for hours. Gathering her closer, he stood.

"It's dangerous to stay in here too long." Briefly he rubbed his mouth against hers. "We'll cool off."

"Impossible," Shelby murmured and lay back against his shoulder. "Absolutely impossible." They left the towels behind.

"The water's cool . . . almost as soft as your skin."

With a half-sigh, she turned to glance at the still surface of the pool. "I can take it if you can." She hooked her arms more securely around his neck. "But I don't think I even have the strength to tread water."

"We'll use the buddy system," Alan suggested, then shifting her weight slightly, jumped in with her.

Shelby gave a quick gasp at the shock of cold, then surfaced, drawing in air and tangling with Alan. "It's freezing!"

"No, actually it's kept at around seventy-six degrees. It's just the abrupt change in temperature."

Shelby narrowed her eyes and splashed water into his face before she broke away to skim along the bottom of the pool. Her muscles felt limber, ready to flex and stretch. When she reached the other end of the pool, Alan was waiting for her.

"Show-off," she accused, tossing wet hair out of her eyes. Then, with her tongue caught between her teeth, she let her gaze roam slowly down him from where the water dripped from his hair to where it lapped gently just below his waist. It didn't matter how many times she saw him, how often she touched, his body would always excite her.

"You look great, Senator. I think I could get used to seeing you wet and naked." Lazily she dipped back to float. "If you ever decide to ditch politics, I imagine you could have a successful career as a lifeguard at a nude beach."

"It's always good to have something to fall back on." He watched her a moment, her body white and smooth against the darker water. Moonlight poured through the windows and shivered on the surface. The desire he'd felt only moments before came back in full force. In one stroke, he was beside her, an arm hooked around her waist. Shelby gripped his shoulders for balance while her head tilted back, her hair streaming into the water. He saw it in her eyes, the excitement, the mutual need. Then her mouth rushed to meet his, and he saw nothing.

She knew there'd be no lazy, patient loving now. His mouth crushed hers, and she tasted the hints of savagery and desperation. The hand at her hip molded her to him. Shelby hadn't known her passion could rise again so swiftly, but it sprang up in her as ripe and hot as before. Desire came in waves, fast, each higher than the one before until she was submerged in it and struggling for air. Their bodies pressed together, wet and urgent. She dove her fingers into his hair, murmuring a thousand promises, a thousand demands.

The water slowed their movements, seeming to tease them when they both would have hurried. Neither had the patience for the dreamlike or the languid now when hunger was so sharp and consuming. She felt the water lap over her shoulders, cool and sensual, while Alan's mouth heated and became more firm, more greedy, on hers. She could smell it on his skin, taste it as her lips trailed over him—that faint trace of chlorine vying with the scent and flavor she had grown so used to. It alone reminded her that they were in a pool and not some sheltered lagoon a thousand miles away.

But when he took her in a frenzy of passion, they might have been anywhere at all.

Chapter Eleven

H_i."

Shelby stifled a yawn as she rounded the last bend in the stairs and caught sight of Serena. "Hi."

"It looks like you and I are the only ones not already involved with some disgustingly productive activity this morning. Had breakfast?"

"Uh-uh." Shelby dropped her hand to her stomach. "I'm starving."

"Good. We usually eat breakfast in a room off the kitchen, as all of us have different hours. Caine," Serena continued as they started down the hall, "is always up at the crack of dawn—a habit I always wanted to strangle him for as a child. Alan and my parents are hardly better. Diana considers 8:00 A.M. late enough for anyone, and Justin runs on a clock I've yet to understand. Anyway, I've got this for an excuse now." She patted her well-rounded stomach.

Shelby grinned. "I don't use any."

"More power to you."

Serena swept into a sun-filled breakfast room that would have been considered large and formal by anything but Daniel MacGregor's standards. Rich royal-blue drapes were tied back from high windows with thick tassels. The carpet was Aubusson in faded blues and golds.

"I can't get over this place." Shelby wandered to a Chippendale server to study a collection of New England pewter.

"Neither can I," Serena said with a laugh. "How do you feel about waffles?"

Shelby grinned over her shoulders. "I have very warm, friendly feelings about waffles."

"I knew I liked you," Serena said with a nod. "Be right back." She disappeared through a side door.

Alone, Shelby wandered, studying a muted French landscape, sniffing fresh flowers in a crystal basket. It would take her all weekend to see every room, she decided. And a lifetime to really appreciate everything in them. Yet she felt at home here, she realized while she stared out the window overlooking the south lawn. She was as comfortable with Alan's family as she was with her own. It should all be so simple for them to love, to marry, to have children.... With a sigh, she rested her forehead against the glass. If it were only so simple for them.

"Shelby?"

Straightening, she turned to see Serena quietly studying her. "I've brought in some coffee," she said after a brief hesitation. She hadn't expected to see those candid gray eyes troubled. "The waffles'll be along in a minute."

"Thanks." Shelby took a seat at the table while Serena poured. "Alan tells me you run a casino in Atlantic City."

"Yes. Justin and I are partners there, and in several other hotels. The rest," she added as she lifted her cup, "he owns alone... for now."

Shelby grinned, liking her. "You'll convince him he needs a partner in the others as well."

"One at a time. I've learned how to handle him rather well the last year or so—especially since he lost the bet and had to marry me."

"You're going to have to clear that one up."

"He's a gambler. So am I. We settled on a flip of a coin." She smiled, remembering. "Heads I win, tails you lose."

Laughing, Shelby set down her cup. "Your coin, I take it."

"You bet your life. Of course he knew, but in all this time, I've never let him see that quarter." In an unconscious gesture, she rested a hand on her stomach. "Keeps him on his toes."

"He's crazy about you," Shelby murmured. "You can see it in the way he looks at you when you walk into a room."

"We've been through a lot, Justin and I." She lapsed into silence a moment, thinking back over the first stormy months after they met, the love that grew despite them, and the fear of making that final commitment. "Caine and Diana too," she went on. "Justin and Diana had a difficult childhood. That made it hard for them to give themselves to a relationship. Strange, I think I loved Justin almost from the start, though I didn't realize it. It was the same for Caine with Diana." She paused, with her warm, candid eyes on Shelby's.

"You MacGregors know your minds quickly."

"I wondered if Alan would ever love anyone, until I saw him with you." She reached across the table to touch Shelby's hand. "I was so glad when I saw you weren't the kind of woman I'd been afraid he'd fall for."

"What kind was that?" Shelby asked with a half-smile.

"Cool, smooth, a sleek blonde perhaps with soft hands and impeccably boring manners." Her eyes lit with humor. "Someone I couldn't bear to have coffee with in the morning."

Though Shelby laughed, she shook her head as she sipped again. "She sounds like someone very suited for Senator Alan MacGregor to me."

"Suited to the title," Serena countered, "not the man. And the man's my brother. He tends to be too serious at times, to work too hard—to care too much. He needs someone to help him remember to relax and to laugh."

"I wish that were all he needed," Shelby said quietly.

Seeing the trouble shadow Shelby's eyes again, Serena felt an instant flood of sympathy. With difficulty, she harnessed it, knowing sympathy too often led to interference. "Shelby, I'm not prying—well, maybe just a bit. I really just wanted you to know how I felt. I love Alan very much."

Shelby stared into her empty cup before lifting her gaze to Serena's. "So do I."

Serena sat back, wishing she could say something wise. "It's never just that easy, is it?"

Shelby shook her head again. "No, no, it's not."

"So, you decided to get up after all." Alan broke the silence as he came through the doorway. Though he noticed something pass between Shelby and his sister, he didn't comment.

"It's barely ten," Shelby stated, tilting back her head for the kiss. "Have you eaten?"

"Hours ago. Any more coffee?"

"Plenty," Serena told him. "Just get a cup from the buffet. Have you seen Justin?"

"Upstairs with Dad."

"Ah, plotting some new brilliant financial scheme."

"Stud poker," Alan corrected as he poured coffee. "Dad's down about five hundred."

"Caine?"

"Down about three."

Serena tried to look disapproving and failed. "I don't know what to do about Justin continuing to fleece my family. How much did you lose?"

Alan shrugged and sipped. "About one seventy-five." Catching Shelby's eye, he grinned. "I only play with Justin for diplomatic reasons." As she continued to stare he leaned back against the buffet. "And, dammit, one day I'm going to beat him."

"I don't believe gambling's legal in this state," Shelby mused, glancing over as the waffles were brought in. "I imagine the fine's rather hefty."

Ignoring her, Alan eyed her plate. "Are you going to eat all those?"

"Yes." Shelby picked up the syrup and used it generously. "Since men's-only clubs are archaic, chauvinistic, and unconstitutional, I suppose I could sit in on a game."

Alan watched the waffles disappear. "None of us has ever considered money has a gender." He twirled one of her curls around his finger. "Are you prepared to lose?"

Shelby smiled as she slipped the fork between her lips. "I don't make a habit of it."

"I believe I'll watch for a bit," Serena considered. "Where are Mom and Diana?"

"In the gardens," Alan told her. "Diana wanted a few tips for the house she and Caine just bought."

"That should give us an hour or two," Serena said with a nod as she rose.

"Doesn't your mother approve of cards?"

"My father's cigars," Serena corrected as they left the room. "He hides them from her—or she lets him think he does."

Remembering Anna's calmly observant eyes, Shelby decided it was probably the latter. Anna, like Alan, would miss little.

As they started up the tower steps Daniel's voice boomed down to them. "Damn your eyes, Justin Blade; you've the luck of the devil."

"Sore losers, those MacGregors," Shelby sighed, sliding her gaze to Alan's.

"We'll see if the Campbells can do any better. New blood," Alan announced from the doorway.

Smoke hung in the air, the rich, fragrant sting of expensive tobacco. They were using Daniel's huge old desk as a table, with chairs pulled up to it. The three men looked over as Shelby and Serena walked in.

"I don't like taking my wife's money," Justin commented, sending her a grin as he clamped a cigar between his teeth.

"You won't have the opportunity of trying." Serena lowered herself to the arm of his chair with a quiet sigh. "Shelby'd like a game or two."

"A Campbell!" Daniel rubbed his hands together. "Aye then, we'll see how the wind blows now. Have a chair, lass. Three raise, ten-dollar limit, jacks or better to open."

"If you think you're going to make up your losses on me, MacGregor," Shelby said mildly as she took her seat, "you're mistaken."

Daniel made a sound of appreciation. "Deal the cards, boy," he ordered Caine. "Deal the cards."

It took less than ten minutes for Shelby to discover that Justin Blade was the best she'd ever come across. And she'd sat at her share of tables—elegant and not so elegant. Daniel played defiantly, Caine with a combination of impulse and skill, but Justin simply played. And won. Because she knew she was up against a more clever gambler than she, Shelby fell back on what she considered her best asset. Blind luck.

Standing idly behind her, Alan watched her discard two hearts, choosing to draw for an inside straight. With a shake of his head, he walked over to the table in the corner to pour himself yet another cup of coffee.

He liked the way she looked, nearly elbow-to-elbow with his father, their fiery heads bent a bit as they studied their cards. It was strange how easily she had slipped into his life, making a quiet splash that promised endless, fascinating ripples. She fit here, in the odd tower room, playing poker with smoke clogging the air and coffee growing cold and bitter in the cups. And she would fit in an elegant Washington function in a room that shone with light and glitter, sipping champagne from a tulip glass.

She fit in his arms at night the way no woman ever had, or would, fit again. Alan needed her in his life as much as he needed food, water, and air.

"A pair of aces," Daniel said with a fierce look in his eye.

Justin set his cards down quietly and faceup. "Two pair. Jacks and sevens." He sat back as Caine swore in disgust.

"You son of—" In frustration, Daniel broke off, shifting his eyes from his daughter to Shelby. "The devil take you, Justin Blade."

"You're sending him off prematurely," Shelby commented, spreading her cards. "A straight, from the five to the nine."

Alan walked over to look at her cards. "I'll be damned, she drew the six and seven."

"No one but a bloody witch draws an inside straight," Daniel boomed, glaring at her.

"Or a bloody Campbell," Shelby said easily.

His eyes narrowed. "Deal the cards."

Justin grinned at her as Shelby scooped in chips. "Welcome aboard," he said quietly and began to shuffle.

They played for an hour, with Shelby sticking to a system of illogic that kept her head above water. Normally she wouldn't have labeled a twenty-five-dollar take impressive, but considering her competition, she was well pleased. Whether they would have played into the afternoon became academic the minute Daniel heard his wife's voice drifting up the stairs. Immediately he stubbed out the better part of a seven-dollar cigar, then shoved it and an ashtray under his desk.

"I'll raise you five," he said, leaning on his desk again.

"You haven't opened yet," Shelby reminded him sweetly. Plucking a peppermint from the bowl on his desk, she popped it into his mouth. "Gotta cover all your tracks, MacGregor."

Daniel grinned and tousled her hair. "A good lass, Campbell or not."

"We should have known they'd be busy losing their money to Justin," Anna stated as she stepped inside the room with Diana beside her.

"Lost a trick to the new kid on the block too." Caine held out a hand for his wife's.

"About time Justin had some competition." Hooking her arms around Caine's neck, Diana rested her chin on the top of his head. "Anna and I were thinking about a swim before lunch. Anyone interested?"

"Fine idea." Daniel eased the ashtray a bit further under his desk with his foot. "Do you swim, girl?"

"Yes." Shelby set down her cards. "But I didn't bring a suit."

"There's a closetful in the bathhouse," Serena told her. "You won't have any trouble finding one to fit."

"Really?" She shot Alan a look. "Isn't that handy? A closetful of suits."

He gave her an easy smile. "Didn't I mention it? A swim sounds good," he added as he dropped his hands to her shoulders. "I've never seen Shelby in a bathing suit.

Twenty minutes later Alan found himself in the relaxing heat of the sauna. Instead of Shelby, he was joined by his brother and Justin. Leaning back, letting his muscles relax, he remembered the damp, soft sheen on her skin and the flush of pink that had covered her when he'd held her.

"I like your taste," Caine commented and rested his shoulders against the side wall. "Even though it surprised me."

Alan opened his eyes enough to bring Caine into focus. "Did it?"

"Your Shelby isn't anything like the classy blonde with the, uh, interesting body you were dating a few months ago." Caine brought up one knee to settle more comfortably. "She wouldn't have lasted five minutes with Dad."

"Shelby isn't like anyone."

"I have to respect someone who draws to an inside straight." Justin added stretching out on his back on the bench above Alan. "Serena tells me she suits you."

"It's always nice to have family approval," Alan said dryly.

Justin only laughed and pillowed his head on his folded arms. "You MacGregors have a habit of interfering in this sort of thing."

"He speaks, of course, from personal experience." Caine pushed damp hair from his forehead. "At the moment, I'm rather enjoying the old man's preoccupation with Alan. It takes the heat off Diana and me."

"You'd think he'd be too involved with Rena and his expected grandchild to put energy into anything else."

Alan rested his arms on the upper bench and let the sweat roll off him.

"Hell, he's not going to be satisfied until he's knee-deep in little MacGregors and/or Blades." Caine grinned. "Actually I've been giving it some thought myself."

"Thinking about it isn't going to produce another Comanche-Scotsman," Justin said lazily.

"Diana and I thought we'd test the waters with our niece or nephew first."

"How does it feel to have fatherhood looming before you, Justin?" Alan asked him.

Justin stared up at the wooden ceiling remembering what it was like to feel life move under his hand, inside the woman he loved. Thrilling. He could see how Serena looked, naked, swollen with his child. Beautiful. He knew how he felt sometimes in the early hours of dawn when she was warm and asleep beside him....

"Terrified," he murmured. "Scares the hell out of me. Babies add a multitude of 'What ifs' to your life. The more I want it, the closer it comes, the more scared I am." He managed to shrug from his prone position. "And the more I want to see just what that part of me and Serena is going to look like."

"Strong stock," Caine stated. "Good blood."

Justin gave a quiet chuckle and closed his eyes. "Apparently Daniel's decided to feel the same way about Campbells. Are you going to marry her, Alan?"

"Here, in the fall."

"Dammit, why didn't you say so?" Caine demanded. "Dad would've had an excuse to dip into that vintage champagne he hoards."

"Shelby doesn't know it yet," Alan said easily. "I thought it wiser to tell her first."

"*Hmm.* She doesn't strike me as a woman who takes to being told."

"Very observant," Alan told Justin. "But then, I've tried asking. Sooner or later I might have to change my tactics."

Caine's brows drew together. "She said no?"

Alan opened his eyes again. "God, there're times you look just like him. She didn't say no—or yes. Shelby's father was Senator Robert Campbell."

"Robert Campbell," Caine repeated quietly. "Oh, I see. She'd have an understandably difficult time with your profession. Her father was campaigning in the presidential primaries when he was assassinated, wasn't he?"

"Yes." Alan read the unspoken question in his brother's eyes. "And yes, I intend to run when the time's right." It was the first time, he realized, that he'd said it out loud. Eight years wasn't so very long to prepare for such a long hard road. He let out a long quiet breath. "It's something else Shelby and I have to discuss."

"You were born for it, Alan," Justin said simply. "It isn't something you can turn your back on."

"No, but I need her. If it came down to making a choice—"

"You'd take Shelby," Caine finished, understanding perfectly what it meant to find one love, one woman. "But I wonder if either of you could live with it."

Alan remained silent a moment, then closed his eyes again. "I don't know." A choice, one way or the other, would split him neatly in two.

On the Wednesday following her weekend in Hyannis Port, Shelby received her first Daniel MacGregor phone call. Holding Auntie Em's water dish in one hand, she picked up the receiver with the other.

"Shelby Campbell?"

"Yes." Her lips curved. No one else boomed at you in quite that way. "Hello, Daniel."

"You've closed down shop for the day?"

"I toss clay on Wednesdays," she told him as she caught the receiver between her ear and shoulder and replaced the bird's water dish. "But yes, I've closed down. How are you?"

"Fine, fine, lass. I'm going to make it a point to take a look at that shop of yours the next time I'm in Washington."

"Good." She dropped to the arm of a chair. "And you'll buy something."

Daniel gave a wheezy chuckle. "That I might, if you're as clever with your hands as you are with your tongue. The family plans to spend the Fourth of July weekend at the Comanche in Atlantic City," Daniel stated abruptly. "I wanted to extend the invitation to you myself."

The Fourth of July, Shelby mused. Fireworks, hot dogs, and beer. It was less than a month away—how had time gone so quickly? She wanted to picture herself standing on the beach with Alan, watching colors explode in the sky. And yet…her future, their future, was something she still couldn't see. "I appreciate it, Daniel. I'd love to come." That much was true, Shelby told herself. Whether she would or not was another matter.

"You're right for my son," Daniel told her, shrewd enough to have caught her brief hesitation. "Never thought I'd hear myself say that about a Campbell, but I'm saying it. You're strong and bright. And you know how to laugh. You've good Scottish blood in you, Shelby Campbell. I'll see it in my grandchildren."

She did laugh, because her eyes had filled too abruptly for her to stop the tears. "You're a pirate, Daniel Mac-Gregor, and a schemer."

"Aye. I'll see you at the Comanche."

"Good-bye, Daniel."

When she hung up, Shelby pressed her fingers to her eyes. She wasn't going to fall apart over a few bluff words. She'd known from the first morning she'd woken in Alan's arms that she was only postponing the inevitable. Right for him? Daniel said she was right for him, but perhaps he only saw the surface. He didn't know what she was holding inside her. Not even Alan knew how deep-seated the fear was, how real and alive it had remained all these years.

If she allowed herself, she could still hear those three quick explosions that had been bullets. And she could see, if she let herself see, the surprised jerk of her father's body, the way he had fallen to the ground almost at her feet. People shouting, rushing, crying. Her father's blood on the skirt of her dress. Someone had pushed her aside to get to him. Shelby had sat on the floor, alone. It had been for perhaps no more than thirty seconds: it had been a lifetime.

She hadn't needed to be told her father was dead—she'd seen the life spill out of him. She'd felt it spill out of herself.

Never again, Shelby thought on a shaky breath. She would never—could never—die so painfully again.

The knock on the door had to be Alan. Shelby gave herself an extra minute to be certain the tears were under control. Taking a last deep breath, she went to answer the door. "Well, MacGregor. No food," she commented with an arched brow. "Too bad."

"I thought his might make up for it." He held out a single rose whose petals were the color of her hair. A traditional gift, she thought, trying to take it casually. But nothing he gave her would ever be taken casually. As her fingers closed around the stem she knew it was a token. A traditional, serious-minded man was offering her a very serious part of himself.

"One rose is supposed to be more romantic than dozens," she said easily enough. Then the tears backed up behind her eyes. It was. "Thank you." She threw her arms around him, pressing her mouth to his with force and a hint of desperation. It was the desperation that had Alan holding her gently, one hand stroking her wild tangle of hair as his lips soothed hers.

"I love you," she whispered, burying her face against his neck until she was certain her eyes were dry.

Alan slipped a hand under her chin to lift it, then studied her. "What's wrong, Shelby?"

"Nothing," she said too quickly. "I get sentimental when someone brings me a present." The quiet intensity in his eyes didn't change; the churning emotion inside her didn't ease. "Make love to me, Alan." She pressed her cheek against his. "Come to bed with me now."

He wanted her. She could make his desire springboard from easy to urgent with a look, but he knew it wasn't the answer either of them needed then. "Let's sit down. It's time we talked."

"No, I—"

"Shelby." He took her by the shoulders. "It's time."

Her breath came out in a jerk. He'd given her all the room he would give her. She'd known he'd draw the line sooner or later. With a nod, she walked to the couch, still clutching the rose. "Would you like a drink?"

"No." With a hand on her shoulder again, he eased her down, then sat beside her. "I love you," he said simply. "You know that and that I want you to marry me. We haven't known each other for long," he continued when Shelby remained silent. "If you were a different kind of woman, I might be persuaded that you needed time to be certain of your feelings for me. But you're not a different kind of woman."

"You know I love you, Alan," she interrupted. "You're going to be logical, and I—"

"Shelby." He could stop an impassioned speech with a whisper. "I know you have a problem with my profession. I understand it, maybe only in a limited way, but I do understand it. It's something you and I have to work out from this point on." He took her hands and felt the tension. "We'll deal with it, Shelby, in whatever way we have to."

She still didn't speak but stared at him as if she already knew what he would say. "I think I should tell you now that I've been approached by a few key members of the party and that I'm seriously considering running for president. It won't be for nearly a decade, but the nuts and bolts of it have already started."

She'd known it—of course she'd known it—but hearing it out loud had the muscles in her stomach contracting like a fist. Feeling the pressure building in her lungs, she let out a long slow breath. "If you're asking my opinion," she managed in a calm voice, "you shouldn't consider it, you should do it. It's something you were meant to do, Alan, something you were meant to be." The words, even as she said them, knew them for the truth, tore at her.

"I know with you, it's not simply a matter of power and ambition. You'd see the hardships as well, the strain, the impossible responsibility." Shelby rose, knowing if she sat still a moment longer, she'd explode. Quickly she set the rose down. Too quickly. The stem nearly snapped between her fingers. "There is such a thing as destiny," she murmured.

"Perhaps." He watched as she paced the room, running her hand over the back of a pillow she snatched from the couch. "You're aware that it's more than just putting my name on the ballot. When the time comes, it'll mean long hard campaigning. I need you with me, Shelby."

She stopped a moment, her back to him, to squeeze her eyes tight. Fighting for composure, she turned around. "I can't marry you, Alan."

Something flashed in his eyes—fury or pain, she couldn't be sure—but his voice was calm when he spoke. "Why?"

Her throat was so dry, she wasn't certain she could answer. With an effort, she swallowed. "You're fond of logic; be logical. I'm not a political hostess; I'm not a diplomat or an organizer. That's what you need."

"I want a wife," Alan returned evenly. "Not a staff."

"Dammit, Alan, I'd be useless. Worse than useless." With a sound of frustration, she began to pace again. "If I tried to fit the mold, I'd go mad. I haven't the patience for beauty shops and secretaries and being tactful twenty-four hours a day. How could I be First Lady when I'm not even a lady half the time?" she tossed out. "And damn you, you'll win. I'd find myself in the White House stifled by elegance and protocol."

He waited as her ragged breathing filled the room. "Are you saying you'd marry me if I chose not to run?"

She whirled around, eyes brilliant and tormented. "Don't do that to me. You'd hate me . . . I'd hate myself. It can't be a choice between what you are and me, Alan."

"But a choice between what you are and me," he countered. The anger he'd strapped in broke free. "You can make a choice." He sprang up from the couch to grab both of her arms. Fury poured out of him, overwhelming her. She'd known it would be deadly, she'd seen hints of it, but she had no defense. "You can choose to push me out of your life with a simple *no*, expect me to accept it knowing you love me. What the hell do you think I'm made of?"

"It's not a choice," she said passionately. "I can't do anything else. I'd be no good for you, Alan; you have to see that."

He shook her with enough violence to snap her head back. "Don't lie to me, and don't make excuses. If you're going to turn your back on me, do it with the truth."

She crumbled so quickly, she would have slid to the floor if he hadn't been holding her. "I can't handle it." Tears streamed down her face, huge, fast, painful. "I can't go through it all again, Alan, waiting, just waiting for someone to—" On a sob, she covered her face with her hands. "Oh, God, please, I can't stand it. I didn't want to love you like this; I didn't want you to matter so much that everything could be taken from me again. I can see it happening all over again. All those people pressing close, all those faces and the noise. I watched someone I love die in front of my eyes once. I can't again; I can't!"

Alan held her close, wanting to soothe, needing to reassure. What words could he use to penetrate this kind of fear, this kind of grief? There was no place for logic here, no place to be calm and rationalize. If it was her love that made her so deadly afraid, how could he ask her to change it?

"Shelby, don't. I won't—"

"No!" She cut him off, struggling out of his hold. "Don't say it. *Don't!* Please, Alan, I can't bear it. You have to be what you are, and so do I. If we tried to change, we wouldn't be the same people each of us fell in love with."

"I'm not asking for you to change," he said evenly as his patience began to strain again. "I'm only asking for you to have faith in me."

"You're asking too much! Please, please just leave me alone." Before he could speak, she dashed into the bedroom and slammed the door.

Chapter Twelve

Maine was beautiful in June—green and wild. Shelby drove along the coast, keeping her mind a blank. Through the open windows of the car, she could hear the water hurl itself against rock. Passion, anger, grief—the sound expressed all three. She understood it.

From time to time there were wildflowers along the roadside, tough little blossoms that could stand up to the salt and the wind. For the most part there were rocks, worn smooth from the eternal beating of water, glistening near the shoreline, dry and brooding above it, until the tide would rise and claim them as well.

If she drew deep, Shelby could breathe again. Perhaps that's why she had come, and come quickly, before Washington could suffocate her. The air here was brisk and clean. The summer that had taken over spring so quickly had yet to reach this far north. She needed to hold on to spring for just a bit longer.

She saw the lighthouse on the narrow point of land that jutted arrogantly into the sea and forced her tense fingers to relax on the wheel. Peace of mind—perhaps she would find it here as her brother always sought to do.

It was barely dawn. When her plane had landed, it had still been dark. She could see the sun rising, streaming color into the sea while gulls dipped and floated over rock and sand and water. It was still too early for their shadows. They called out above the noise of the surf, an empty, lonely sound. Shelby shook that off. She wouldn't think of emptiness or loneliness now. She wouldn't think at all.

The beach was deserted, the air cool and breezy when she stepped from her car. The lighthouse was a wide sphere of white, solitary and strong against the elements. Perhaps it was worn and a bit weather-beaten in places, but it held a simple power that remained timeless and real. It seemed a good place to shelter from any storm.

Shelby took her bag from the back of the car and approached the door at the base. It would be locked, she knew. Grant never gave open invitations. She pounded on the wood with the side of her fist, wondering just how long he'd ignore it before answering. He'd hear it, because Grant heard everything, just as he saw everything. Isolating himself from the rest of humanity hadn't changed that.

Shelby pounded again and watched the sun rise. It took a bit more than five full minutes before the door creaked open.

He had the look of their father, Shelby thought—dark, intelligent good looks, a bit rough around the edges. The surprisingly deep green eyes were clouded with sleep, the thick just-a-bit-too-long hair, rumpled with it.

Grant scowled at her and rubbed a hand over his unshaven chin. "What the hell are you doing here?"

"A typical Grant Campbell welcome." She stood on her toes to brush his lips with hers.

"What time is it?"

"Early."

Swearing, he dragged a hand through his hair and stepped back to let her through. For a moment, he leaned against the door to get his bearings, one thumb hooked in his only concession to modesty—a pair of faded cutoffs.

Then he followed her up the steep, creaky flights of stairs to his living quarters.

Straightening, he took his sister by the shoulders and studied her, quickly, and with an intensity she had never quite grown used to. She stood passively, a half-smile on her lips and shadows under her eyes.

"What's wrong?" he asked bluntly.

"Wrong?" She shrugged and tossed her bag on a chair that could have done with reupholstering. "Why does there have to be something wrong for me to pay a visit?" She glanced back at him, noting that he still hadn't put on any weight. His build teetered between lean and thin, and yet, like his home, there was a basic strength about him. She needed that too. "You gonna make the coffee?"

"Yeah." Grant moved through what served as a living room, despite the dust, and into a tidy, organized kitchen. "Want breakfast?"

"Always."

With what might have been a chuckle, he pulled out a slab of bacon. "You're skinny, kid."

"You're not exactly husky these days yourself."

His answer was a grunt. "How's Mom?"

"She's fine. I think she's going to marry the Frenchman."

"Dilleneau, with the big **ears** and the cagey brain."

"That's the one." Shelby dropped into a chair at the round oak table as bacon began to sizzle. "Are you going to immortalize him?"

"Depends." He shot Shelby a wicked grin. "I don't suppose Mom would be surprised to see her fiancé in Macintosh."

"Surprised, no—pleased..." She trailed off with a shrug. "She'd really like you to come down for a visit."

"Maybe." Grant plopped a plate of bacon on the table.

"Are we going to have eggs too?" She got up for plates and mugs while Grant broke a half-dozen into a pan. "Sure, scrambled's fine," Shelby said wryly to his back. "Getting many tourist these days?"

"No."

The word was so flat and final, Shelby nearly laughed. "You could always try land mines and barbed wire. It amazes me how anyone so in tune with people could dislike them so much."

"I don't dislike them." Grant heaped eggs on another plate. "I just don't want to be around them." Without standing on ceremony, he sat down and began to fill his plate. He ate; Shelby pretended to. "How're your roommates?"

"They've settled on peaceful coexistence," Shelby told him as she nibbled on a slice of bacon. "Kyle's looking in on them until I get back."

Grant shot her a look over the rim of his mug. "How long are you staying?"

This time she did laugh. "Always gracious. A few days," she told him. "No more than a week. No, please." She held up her hand, palm up. "Don't beg me to extend my visit; I simply can't stay any longer." She knew he would scowl and swear and open his home to her for as long as she needed.

He finished off the last of his eggs. "Okay, you can drive into town for supplies while you're here."

"Always happy to be of service," Shelby muttered. "How do you manage to get every major newspaper in the country delivered out here?"

"I pay for it," he said simply. "They think I'm odd."

"You are odd."

"Just so. Now..." He pushed his plate aside and leaned his elbows on the table. "Why are you here, Shelby?"

"I just wanted to get away for a few days," she began, only to be cut off by a rude four-letter word. Instead of responding with a joke or an equally rude rejoinder, she dropped her gaze to her plate. "I had to get away," she whispered. "Grant, my life's a mess."

"Whose isn't?" he responded, but put one long slender finger under her chin to lift it. "Don't do that, Shelby," he murmured when he saw her eyes were brimming over. "Take a deep breath and tell me about it."

She took the breath, though it was a shaky one, and struggled to control the tears. "I'm in love and I shouldn't be, and he wants me to marry him and I can't."

"Well, that sums things up. Alan MacGregor." When Shelby sent him a swift look, Grant shook his head. "No, no one told me. You've been linked with him in the papers half a dozen times in the last month. Well, he's one of that tidy little group I can honestly say I respect."

"He's a good man," Shelby stated, blinking back tears. "Maybe a great one."

"So what's the problem?"

"I don't want to love a great man," she said fiercely. "I can't marry one."

Grant rose, retrieved the coffeepot, and filled both mugs again. He sat, then pushed the cream at Shelby. "Why?"

"I won't go through it again, Grant."

"Through what?"

Her look sharpened; the tears dried up. "Damn you, don't pull that on me."

Calmly he sipped his coffee, pleased that she would snipe at him now rather than weep. "I've been hearing a rumor or two that the Senator might try for the top spot sooner or later. Maybe sooner than expected.''

"You hear correctly, as usual."

He lingered over the coffee, black and strong. ''Don't you fancy having one of your dresses in the Smithsonian, Shelby?''

"Your humor's always been on the odd side, Grant."

"Thanks."

Annoyed, she pushed her plate aside. ''I don't want to be in love with a senator.''

"Are you?" he countered. "Or are you in love with the man?"

"It's the same thing!"

"No, it's not." He set down the coffee and plucked a piece of untouched bacon from Shelby's plate. ''You, better than most, know it.''

"I can't risk it!" she said with sudden passion. "I just can't. He'll win, Grant, he will if he lives long enough. I can't deal with it—the possibilities..."

"You and your possibilities," he flung back. The memory hurt, but he pushed it aside. "Okay, let's take a few of them. First, do you love him?"

"Yes, yes, I love him. Dammit, I just told you I did."

"How much does he mean to you?"

Shelby dragged both hands through her hair. ''Everything.''

"Then, if he runs for president and something happens to him..." He paused as the color drained from her face. "Is it going to hurt any less whether you have his ring on your finger or not?"

"No." She covered her mouth with her hand. "Don't, Grant."

"You've got to live with it," he said harshly. "We've both had to live with it, carry it around with us. I was there, too, and I haven't forgotten. Are you going to shut yourself off from life because of something that happened fifteen years ago?"

"Haven't you?"

Direct hit, he thought ruefully, but didn't acknowledge it. "We're not talking about me. Let's take another of your possibilities, Shelby. Suppose he loves you enough to chuck it for you."

"I'd despise myself."

"Exactly. Now, the last one. Suppose..." And for the first time he linked his hand with hers. "He runs and wins and lives to a ripe old age writing his memoirs and traveling as an ambassador of goodwill or playing Parcheesi on the sun porch. You're going to be damned mad he had fifty years without you."

She let out a long breath. "Yeah. But—"

"We've already gone through the buts," he interrupted. "Of course, there're probably several million possibilities in between. He could get hit by a car crossing the street—or you could. He could lose the election and become a missionary or an anchor on the six o'clock news."

"All right." Shelby dropped her forehead to their joined hands. "Nobody makes me see what a fool I am better than you."

"One of my minor talents. Listen, walk out on the beach; clear your head. When you come back, eat something, then get about twelve-hours sleep, because you look like hell. Then..." He waited until she lifted her head to smile at him. "Go home. I've got work to do."

"I love you, you creep."

"Yeah." He shot her one of his quick grins. "Me too."

His house was too empty and too quiet, but there was nowhere Alan wanted to go. He'd forced himself to give Shelby a full day alone, then had gone half mad when he'd learned on Friday that she was nowhere to be found. Twenty-four hours later, he was still trying to reason with himself.

She had a right to go when and where she chose. He had no reason to expect her to answer or to explain to him. If she decided to go off for a few days, he had no right to be angry, certainly no reason to be worried.

He rose from the desk in his study to pace. Where the hell was she? How long was she going to stay away? Why hadn't she at least let him know?

Frustrated, he balled his hands into his pockets. He'd always been able to find the route out of a problem. If it didn't work one way, it worked another, but there was always a viable system. It was only a matter of time and patience. He had no more patience. He was hurting like he'd never been aware he could hurt—everywhere, all at once, and unrelentingly.

When he found her, he'd... What? Alan demanded of himself. Force her, bully her, plead, beg? What was left? He could give up pieces of himself for her and still be whole, but without her, he'd never be more than part of a man. She'd stolen something from him, then shut the door, he thought furiously. No... He'd given it to her freely, though she'd been reluctant to take the love he offered. He couldn't take it back now, even if she disappeared from his life.

She was capable of that, he realized with a sudden surge of panic. Shelby could pack her bags and take off without leaving a trace behind. Damn if she would! Alan frowned at the phone again. He'd find her. First he'd find her. Then he'd deal with her, one way or another.

He'd start by calling her mother, then work his way through everyone she knew. With a brittle laugh, Alan picked up the receiver. With Shelby, it could take the better part of a week.

Before he could dial, the doorbell sounded. Alan let it ring three times before he remembered that McGee was in Scotland. Swearing, he slammed down the phone and went to answer.

The messenger grinned at him. "Delivery for you, Senator," he said brightly and handed Alan a clear plastic bag. "You guys are strange," he added before he sauntered away. While he stared at the bag in his hand, Alan closed the door. Swimming around a bit frantically in the trapped water was a bright-orange goldfish.

Slowly Alan moved into the parlor, studying his gift with wary eyes. What the hell was he supposed to do with this? he wondered. Impatient with the interruption, he pulled out a Waterford goblet and breaking the seal on the plastic, dumped fish and water inside. After setting the bag aside, Alan opened the little card that had been attached to it.

Senator,
    If you can take life in the goldfish bowl, so can I.

After reading the one sentence three times, Alan shut his eyes. She'd come back. The card dropped to the table as he turned to head for the door. Even as he opened it, the doorbell rang.

"Hi." Shelby smiled, though the greeting had been bright enough to reveal her nerves. "Can I come in?"

He wanted to grab her quickly, hold her to be sure she stayed. It wasn't the way to keep Shelby. "Sure." When he wanted to step forward, Alan stepped back to let her come in on her own. "You've been away."

"Just a quick pilgrimage." She thrust her hands into the wide pockets of a pair of baggy denim overalls. He looked tired, she noted, as if he hadn't slept. Her hands itched to touch his face, but she kept them both firmly tucked away.

"Come in and sit down." Alan gestured toward the parlor before they walked, both cautious and conscious of the other. "McGee's away. I could fix coffee."

"No, not for me." Shelby wandered the room. How was she going to start? What was she going to say? All the careful speeches, the glib ones, the passionate ones, slipped quietly out of her head. He'd placed the krater she'd made him near the window where it caught the sun. She stared at it. "I suppose I should begin by apologizing for falling apart on you the other day.

"Why?"

"Why?" Shelby turned around to face him again. "Why what?"

"Why would you apologize?"

She lifted her shoulders, then let them fall. "I hate to cry. I'd rather swear, or kick something." Nerves were jumping inside her—something she hadn't expected, and something his calm, steady gaze did nothing to soothe. "You're angry with me."

"No."

"You were." She moved restlessly around the room. "You had a right to be, I . . ." Shelby trailed off when she spotted the goldfish swimming in circles inside the Waterford. "Well, he's come up in the world," she said with a jerky laugh. "I don't think he appreciates it. Alan." When she faced him this time, her eyes were huge and questioning and vulnerable. "Do you still want me? Have I ruined it?"

He would have gone to her then, taken her on any terms—hers or his. But he wanted more than the moment, much more.

"Why did you change your mind?"

Shelby went toward him, grabbing his hands. "Does it matter?"

"It matters." He released her hands only to frame her face with his own. His eyes held that brooding serious look that could still turn her knees to jelly. "I have to know you'll be happy; have what you want, what you can live with. I want forever from you."

"All right." Shelby lifted her hands to his wrists, holding them a moment before she backed away. "I considered the possibilities," she began. "I thought through all the ifs and the maybes. I didn't like all of them, but the one I hated the most was life without you. You're not going to play Parcheesi without me, MacGregor."

His brow lifted. "I'm not?"

"No." She brushed at her bangs with another unsteady laugh. "Marry me, Alan. I won't agree with all your policies, but I'll try to be tactful in print—some of the time. I won't head any committees, and I'll only go to luncheons if there's no way out, but my own career's an understandable excuse for that. I won't give conventional parties, but I'll give interesting ones. If you're willing to take the risk of setting me loose on world politics, who am I to argue?"

He hadn't thought he could love her any more than he already did. He'd been wrong. "Shelby, I could go back to law, open a practice right here in Georgetown."

"No!" She whirled away from him. "No, dammit, you're not going back to law, not for me, not for anyone! I was wrong. I loved my father, I adored him, but I can't let what happened to him control the rest of my life—or yours." She stopped, needed to control her voice to calmness again. "I'm not changing for you, Alan. I can't. But I can do what you asked and have faith in you." She shook her head before he could speak. "I won't pretend that I won't ever be frightened, or that there won't be parts of the way we live that I'll hate. But I'll be proud of what you do." Calmer, she turned back to him. "I'm proud of who you are. If I still have a few dragons to fight, Alan, I'll do it."

He came to her, looking into her eyes before he gathered her close. "With me?"

She let out a long relieved sigh. "Always." When she turned her head, her mouth found his as hungry and seeking as her own. She felt it had been years rather than days and urged him down, with a murmur of his name, on the carpet with her.

There was no patience in either of them, only needs. Alan swore, fighting with snaps until Shelby laughed and rolled atop him to drive him senseless with her lips on his naked chest. He wasn't content only to be touched. His hands sought her through the denim, causing her strength to sag and her brain to cloud.

When at last there were no more obstructions, he added his mouth to his hands, devouring and molding. The house was silent except for breathless murmurs and quiet sighs.

Once more he buried his face in her hair to absorb the fragrance, to let it absorb him, as Shelby drew him into her.

Then there was nothing but pleasure, the desperate, whirling pleasure of being together.

It was late afternoon with softening light when Shelby stirred against him. They lay together on the couch, tangled and naked and drowsy. A bottle of wine grew warm on the table beside them.

When she opened her eyes, she saw that he slept on, his face relaxed, his breathing even. Here was the contentment, the easy, solid contentment she felt each time she lay quiet in his arms. Tilting her head back, Shelby watched him until he, too, stirred and his eyes opened. With a smile, she leaned closer to touch her lips to his.

"I can't remember when I've spent a more...enjoyable Saturday." She sighed, then teased his tongue with hers.

"Since I don't intend to move for at least twenty-four hours, we'll see how you like Sunday as well."

"I think I'm going to love it." She slid a hand over his shoulder. "I don't like to be pushy, Senator, but when are you going to marry me?"

"I thought September in Hyannis Port."

"The MacGregor fortress." He saw by her eyes the idea appealed to her. "But September's two and a half months away."

"We'll make it August," he said as he nibbled at her ear. "In the meantime, you and your roommates can move in here, or we can start looking for another place. Would you like to honeymoon in Scotland?"

Shelby nestled into his throat. "Yes." She tilted her head back. "In the meantime," she said slowly as her hands wandered down to his waist. "I've been wanting to tell you that there's one of your domestic policies I'm fully in favor of, Senator.''

"Really?" His mouth lowered to hover just above hers.

"You have—" she nipped at his bottom lip "—my full support. I wonder if you could just...run through the procedure for me one more time.''

Alan slid a hand down her side. "It's my civic duty to make myself available to all my constituents.''

Shelby's fingers ran up his chest to stop his jaw just before he captured her lips. "As long as it's only me, Senator.'' She hooked her arm around his neck. "This is the one-man one-vote system.''

*   *   *   *   *

Shelby's brother, Grant Campbell, was a loner—
until Genevieve knocked on his lighthouse door.
Look for ONE MAN'S ART,
Language of Love #17.

COMING NEXT MONTH!

If you enjoyed reading about the tempestuous MacGregor clan, here's great news: the MacGregor saga continues next month in Nora Roberts' moving love story of how it all began in *For Now, Forever*, Volume #19.

Readers begged for the story of how Daniel MacGregor, founder of the MacGregor dynasty, first wooed and won the unflappable Anna Whitfield. You know Daniel as an inveterate matchmaker—see what happens when he meets his own match! In the battle between proud, independent Anna and arrogant, ambitious Daniel, love is the conqueror.

For Now, Forever, the fifth exciting book in the MacGregor series, will move you to laughter and tears—and it's coming your way next month!

THE LANGUAGE of LOVE